# If I Walked In Her Shoes
## Reflections in Caregiving

### A Novel By

### Susan Salach

PRESS

*If I Walked In Her Shoes*
*Reflections in Caregiving*
by Susan Salach

Printed in the United States of America

ISBN 978-1-60647-613-0

www.xulonpress.com

*This book is dedicated to those special people
who made the choice to care for an aging loved one.
Thank you for making a difference every day
by taking on the difficult role of caregiver
and offering love and support
to enhance the quality of their life.*

*May you be blessed as you have been a blessing to others.*

# PROLOGUE
# Care Giving

The *National Family Caregiver Association* estimates that there are currently over *50 million* family caregivers in the United States. Of those, 20 million are part of what is referred to as the *Sandwich Generation.* This means that they are the "meat in the sandwich," providing care for both their children and their parents or grandparents. As the Baby Boomer Generation grows older the number of caregivers will increase in the years to come.

This Sandwich Generation faces a number of special challenges in caregiving, especially when an aging loved one moves into the family home. Caregivers are constantly being pulled from both ends of the generational spectrum — below and above:

- *From below:* Their own children — whether toddlers, teens, or young adults — require a lot of time and attention from their parents as they grow and face new trials and opportunities.
- *From above:* Their aging parents require time and attention as well.

Those sandwiched in the middle can easily become overwhelmed trying to meet the physical, psycho-social, and emotional needs of both their children and their aging loved ones.

Ephesians 6:2-3 (NIV) exhorts us: "'Honor your father and mother'"—which is the first commandment with a promise—"'that it may go well with you and that you may enjoy long life on the earth.'"

That is quite a promise.

We all want to enjoy long life on the earth. What happens, however, when the commitment to honoring our parent's leads us to feel guilty or make poor decisions based on self-reproach or lack of information and resources? Or what if we are in the bind between doing what's best for our aging parents or our young children?

Caregivers can readily become taskmasters who work through their *To-Do* lists for their children and parents. The Bible is very clear about the promise, but what we need to be clear about is exactly what *honoring* truly means. Many take this as a mandate always to move the aging parent into their home.

In some cases this *will be* how we honor them. But in other cases we may better honor our parents by securing an Independent or Assisted Living community to enable and empower them to remain as independent as they possibly can and afford them opportunities for social interaction with a cohort of others who are experiencing the same types of issues and losses in their lives.

Moving an aging loved one into our home is not always a bad idea. If our parents need care we are called to assist them. We are expected to help. Nevertheless, there are times when these decisions are made in haste or without a full knowledge of how these arrangements will affect our relationship with that loved one.

The reality is that caring for an elderly parent can be both challenging and rewarding. It can be the greatest blessing and the most painful ordeal that a person may ever experience. The good news is that there are more options and resources available today to help us care for older adults—to help us truly honor our parents—than at any time in history. Providing care for our aging parents entails:

- **Multitasking:** coordinating doctor appointments, customizing areas of our home to accommodate any physical disabilities or other special needs, physically caring for them with such tasks as bathing and dressing, which can lead to uncomfortable situations, etc.
- **Changes in family dynamics:** Changes in family dynamics are inevitable when Sandwich Generation parents are simultaneously providing care for their own children and their own parents and when grandchildren's lives change to accommodate or help care for a grandparent. Competing demands for such limited resources as time and energy—and possibly even material things—can create tension and conflict.

Having acknowledged all that, there is something—some*one*—else we need to consider. It is the other side of the story; a different perspective—the perspective of the aging loved one.

As caregivers we must always remember that older adults do not wake up one day and say, "Boy, am I getting old! I think I will go live with my children and change the dynamics of our relationship, completely throw their well-established daily routine off-kilter due to the extra time and effort they will have to spend meeting my growing physical needs."

It's not as if they plan to one day have some kind of illness or accident that will cause them to lose their independence and be forced to live with their children. This is not the eternal hope of older adults.

Quite the opposite.

The great majority of these older adults have led lives that were about giving—not taking. They have given to their families, taken care of others. The last thing they want to be is a burden to those they love! They have hoped to remain as independent as possible to continue caring for others until the very end. Almost always it is some type of loss that drives aging parents to have to move into their children's homes. A loss of some capacity—mental or physical—that prevents them from being able to fully care for themselves.

The emotional toll is often severe. Therefore, caregivers must avoid focusing all of their attention on information and resources for addressing physical needs (e.g., activities of daily living, grooming, bathing, eating, and dressing). There is a whole other category of issues that often goes unnoticed—the emotional and psycho-social issues: issues of loss of a spouse and friends, of a family home in which they may have lived for most of their life and raised their family, of the ability to care for themselves.

*If I Walked In Her Shoes* will give you a firsthand look at these dynamics by inviting you to spend a day with two very different, yet very similar people: Rose, the elderly mother, and Sara, her dutiful daughter.

Rose and Sara exemplify these issues. You will see how their day parallels in time, but not in activity. You will experience their struggles, triumphs, and the underlying love that is the foundation of their relationship.

# Sara's Journal

## Monday 12/3

B reaking News!!! Glass ceiling no more. Yours truly is about to be named Vice President of Olson Industries. Me, little old Sara Chapin, a VP of a Fortune 1500 company? Stan Westin told me today that my promotion would be announced at the company's quarterly meeting in January. Steve called three times to see if there was any news, and when I finally got back to the office and called to tell him he started crying. What a wonderful man!!! And he's lucky, too, to be married to a corporate executive : ) I am so thankful (thank you, Lord!)—but having worked so hard and made so many sacrifices, all those 12-hour days…it's nice to see they weren't in vain. VP!

## Sunday 12/9

Today is the third anniversary of Dad's passing. Tough day. A lot of tears. After church, Steve and Tommy and I drove over to spend the day with Mom. We had a late lunch then went to the cemetery and put a poinsettia on Dad's grave and paid our respects. I know he's smiling down on Mom, the love of his life. She took such wonderful care of him for those last five years when his mind and health were failing. I was so scared she would fall apart after he passed—then when she didn't, I got a little bummed about it. They had been together for 55 years. Mom actually comforted <u>me</u>. Does she ever get sad about it? She hugged me and said, "We'll see him again, Sara. He's in heaven now waiting for us and he'll know who we are again when we get there."

She is enjoying life again. I miss you, Daddy.

**Tuesday 12/11**

Tommy is in his high school's production of "A Christmas Carol." He is the Ghost of Christmas Past. We're so proud of him. He's really buckled down in his senior year and turned a big, sharp corner. He is already making a short list of colleges he's interested in. Sally called to say she would be coming home from college for Christmas after all! Her roommate's parents postponed the Caribbean cruise till spring break. She is 6 credits short of being a junior! Go girl!

**Saturday 12/16**

Tommy had dress rehearsal for the play and went out for pizza with Lisa (his new girlfriend), so Steve and I had a romantic candlelight dinner of our own at Ruggierio's Ristorante. Hard to believe we're just a little over a year away from being empty-nesters! Ah! It's so scary and so exciting all at once. Things have come together so well. Sally's doing great at college. Tommy's on the straight and narrow (thank you, Lord!). Steve and I have reached a stretch of the career path that will give us more time to travel. We are blessed. Life is sweet.

**Sunday 12/24**

We all went to Mom's for Christmas Eve. She is getting along so well. I hope I'm as independent as she is when I'm three score and twenty! Wait, that's four-score. Mom is

80?!*! She's become quite the social bee and has so much buzzing for the holiday season it's a wonder she could work us in! I do wish that once in a while she could show that she misses Daddy. That's a weird thing to think, but it's true. Back to the story.... The house was beautiful. Every last ornament was out (even that reindeer with three antlers!) and the house looked just like I remember it from childhood. Mom and Dad bought the house when Mom was pregnant with Carol and it really is a "family home" in the best sense of the word. We lit a candle for Dad, said a prayer of thanksgiving, and agreed that we all have so much to be thankful for this Christmas. We are blessed....

**Monday 1/1**

Happy New Year! Steve and I went out and rang in the new year at a smokin' hot jazz club downtown. Can you believe it? We bought a new calendar to X off the days to our cruise in September...we're going to ALASKA!!! Oh, and last night we discovered that we can still dance! And we resolved that we would dance more in the coming year—a lot more. We're going to get back to ballroom dancing. Remember when? We used to do a mean tango. Our joint resolutions were to learn to play golf and get back to dancing. Hey, we have to do something in our empty-nest years! Bottoms up on the mineral water: Here's to a great year.

**Friday 1/16**

Today was the big day. Q1 company meeting. I was named VP and got a standing ovation. To be honest, it was a little embarrassing. I'm so not used to being the center of attention and having people sing my praises. I made it through the whole ceremony without shedding a tear. Executives don't cry...until they get back into the privacy of their office, that is. I cried buckets. I wish Daddy were here to see it. I think he would have been very proud of his little princess. Mom made reservations for the five of us (Sally's coming home for the weekend!) at the Green Room for tomorrow night to celebrate.

### Friday 2/9

The executive conference is less than two weeks away. Still so much to do. Steve and I have a date at 7:30 tomorrow morning at the River Pines indoor driving range for golf lessons and lunch at the Tenth Hole, then I have to head over to the office and work on the conference. Mom called this afternoon. She's going to Joliet with a church group next week for a Helping Hands mission trip. Said she turned her left ankle moving the living room sofa (Steve said he's going to kill her for not calling him!) but she's just icing it to keep the swelling down and walking softly (but still carrying a big stick : ).

### Monday 2/12

Not a good day. I was in a meeting with Rich Canter, manager at the Hotel Internationale, working out the final details for the executive conference we're hosting next week when my cell phone rang. Didn't recognize the number, so I let the voicemail catch it. The fourth time it rang, I excused myself and answered. It was Mary, Mom's next-door neighbor, saying "Rose has fallen in her bathroom and the paramedics just got here." I held the line for a few minutes until the lead paramedic came on the line and told me that they were transporting Mom to NorthStar General for x-rays. He couldn't say whether there was a fracture. I told Rich I would be back in an hour or two. I really didn't think it was as bad as it turned out to be.

I went to the ER at NorthStar and the charge nurse "briefed" me on Mom's condition. She slipped on the throw rug in her hall bathroom and fell against the bathtub and fractured her hip. They're not sure how long she lay there before she managed to crawl to the kitchen and call Mary. Thank God Mom had given Mary a key; she called 911 then went over and waited with Mom till the paramedics arrived.

The nurse showed me back to Mom's room. On the way back I heard moaning and groaning and crying. A woman was screaming, "Help me, please, somebody help me!" I couldn't believe that it was Mom. I tried to get her calmed down, but she was so confused I'm not even sure she recognized me at first. It was so unreal. For a moment there I felt like I was seeing Daddy a year or two into his Alzheimer's.... It scared me. I asked the charge nurse if she had hit her head in the fall. She said they had ruled out a head injury and that confusion was a common after-effect of trauma for the elderly. I wanted to tell her that she didn't know my mom and how strong she was, how sound her mind was. I guess it was the pain medication they gave her...?

Steve met me at the hospital and tried his best to cheer Mom up with his charm before they wheeled her to the OR so they could set her hip. It sort of worked. She's always been so crazy about him. She made it through the surgery fine, but will some need some physical therapy.

Needless to say I never made it back to the hotel. The conference is next weekend, so I am seriously behind now. I'll make it up with a long day tomorrow. And it's past my bedtime....

### Friday 2/17

What a week. I think I've managed to get 8 hours of sleep...in the past five days. If all goes well, they are going to release Mom on Monday morning. Thank God, most of her confusion has cleared up, and the doctor said she is doing "better than expected." I'm always leery of that line, but I'll take it at face value for the time being. She will have to go to an in-patient rehab center for the first several weeks where they can do intensive therapy—three or four sessions a day.

She is very weak. It is as though the past week has aged her 20 years. Sally (who drove in from college) and Tommy were both shocked and wondered whether Grandma had suffered a head injury in the fall. They are so used to seeing Mom as the strong matriarch. If I know Mom, though, she's a fighter. She'll be up and around in no time.

I hope. And pray.

Steve has been such a godsend. He's so fond of Mom, and his schedule is so much more flexible than mine (hey, wait a minute, I am the VP; what's wrong with that picture?), so he was able to keep Mom company a lot this week so I could put in some 14-hour days to finish planning the executive conference. It's all set. Hope I haven't forgotten anything.

Now we have some decisions to make—and quick!—about which rehab center is best for Mom. It's 1 a.m. I have to get to bed. Tomorrow is another day. Oops, I wonder if Steve remembered to cancel our 8 a.m. golf lesson tomorrow....

**Saturday 2/18**

Gloomy day—cold, gray, and sleeting. We met with the patient advocate and staff social worker at NorthStar this morning and went over our options for rehab centers. They suggested that we involve Mom as much as possible in the decision-making, but she didn't seem the least bit interested in it. I think she suspects we are going to have her "committed" to a nursing home against her will. After an hour and a half, Steve and I had a list of facilities to visit but more questions than answers. It seems like there would be a resource guide to help people make these decisions.

I called Carol and asked her opinion. Surprise, surprise: she had more advice to dispense than Dear Abby. She always does. I'm being sarcastic and I pray the Lord will work it out of me. It's just that she's off in la-la land (a/k/a southern California) with her husband and kids and life and here we are stuck having to...enough said. She's my big sister, and I love her, but she infuriates me. She said that she would try to get back here late Spring…. They're taking the kids to Cabo San Lucas for Spring Break. Yee. ha.

Anyway, Steve and I spent the late morning and early afternoon criss-crossing the county to visit the "top four" facilities, but by the time we made it across the lobby of the third one we had concluded that they were all pretty much the same. We didn't even know what questions to ask. In the end, we settled on The Albright Center, the one closest to our home, so we can run over and see Mom on the way home from work. It was reasonably bright and cheery in the physical therapy unit, which had skylights in the ceiling.

### Sunday 2/19

We slept in this morning—all the way to 8 a.m.…when the hospital called to say that Mom had an urgent matter to discuss with me. We threw on some clothes, told Tommy to tell everybody at church where we were, and headed over to NorthStar. Mom wanted to know what "home" she was going to be put in. I explained that it wasn't a "home" but a reha-bilitation center where she was going for physical therapy that would enable her to pick up where she left off. She was skeptical about it. She said she wasn't born yesterday…. Steve chimed in and helped put her mind at ease—a little bit—telling her that the place was practically the Waldorf Astoria. She said, "I'll expect concierge service then."

When I told her that we had reserved a room for her at the Albright Center, she said, "I told you I wanted to go to Pemberton." Ugh. That's where Daddy spent the last year of his life—in the unit for the "memory impaired." I honestly don't remember her ever saying that's where she wanted to go. Steve said he thought he remembered her saying some-thing about going where Jack was, but I think he was just covering for her. He certainly never said anything of the sort to me when we were driving around all day visiting the places. Anyway, I said, "Mom, why would you want to go there? Besides, Albright is closer to us, so we'll be able to visit more often."

She started crying then, saying, "Just put me where you want me and make it easy on yourself."

I couldn't believe it. What has happened here? I feel as if someone has taken my mom and left me with a woman I don't even know. What a difference a week makes. I can't believe she would want to go to Pemberton. There are so many sad memories there. Why would she want to put herself—and the rest of us—through that? Steve was no help here. He said, "If she wants to go to Pemberton, then she should be able to go to Pemberton." Pemberton is a <u>NURSING HOME</u>. Come on, people! It does have a nicely remodeled rehab unit where the goal is to get the people back home, however; that's not what it's all about.

Steve even suggested that maybe <u>I</u> am the one who has the problem with Pemberton because it was where daddy died...well, where my <u>father</u> died. Daddy was gone a long time before we put him in Pemberton. Enough for now. I don't need to go there. P.S.: I can't remember the last time I wrote a two-page journal entry. I have to have some way to deal with all this.

### Monday 2/20

Pemberton it is. I took half a day off and signed a mound of paperwork to get Mom into Pemberton. Ugh! It is so hard for me to walk into the building.Steve and I were wrong: These places are <u>not all alike</u>. I can't help it; I just feel an ache in my soul when I walk into that place. It's like visiting Daddy's grave every day. But, like Steve said, *I'm* not the one who has to live there for a month—Mom is. Speaking of which, after the orthopedist Dr. Peterson finished Mom's discharge paperwork, I asked him how long he thought Mom's rehab might take. He gave me a look as if I had grown a third eye and fourth ear and said, "A long time." I said, "Weeks, months, what are we talking about?" He said, "It depends." I hate that answer. I have always hated that answer—ever since I was a little girl! I would take any answer over that no matter what the question was.

Steve came to the doctor's rescue. He said later that he could see that fire in my eyes and wanted to spare the good doctor a good drubbing. What it all boiled down to is, the chance that Mom will be able to pick up where she left off last week when she fell is slim…to none. At her age, a severe fracture is likely to lead to permanent "impairment in her mobility." And the recovery time is long because her body does not have the self-healing capacity it once had. And even with all the physical therapy, she probably will lose a lot of strength in the muscles she is no longer using.

Depressing. I felt like I was flashing back to that day they told us that Daddy's mind was deteriorating—only now they were telling me that Mom's body was going and there was little we could do to stop it.Lord have mercy.

I canceled the dance class and golf lessons we had scheduled. Postponed them anyway. Maybe in a few months when things settle down we'll be able to pick them up....

### Monday 2/27

Things have settled down a little. We're getting into a routine. Somewhat. Steve has been having breakfast with Mom every morning at Pemberton, and I have been visiting her in the evenings. I try to make it in time for dinner with her, but most nights it's been a little later because my workload has been a real bear (what's new?). We have signed on with a new health insurance carrier and Stan, the CEO, appointed me to chair the task-force for implementing the new employee benefits package. I would say I feel honored, but that is one part of Human Resources that has never appealed to me.

Mom seems to be adjusting to the place a whole lot better than I am. I just can't manage to get past my grief when I enter that place—the sight of it, the smell of it, the sound of it. The name—Pemberton—makes me want to cry every time I think of it.Each time I walk in there I can't stop the overwhelming feeling of sadness, the same way I did when we first "put" Daddy there.The staff is so nice to me when I visit, and the unit Mom is on is strictly for short-term patients who are there to get better and go home, but I can't get beyond the thought that this was the last place my father "lived."

# Chapter One

# 3 a.m.

S ara woke up with a jolt, raised up on her elbows, eyes wide open, mind racing with the haunting thought *du jour*: *I forgot to fill Mom's pill case.*

The clock radio read 3 a.m., though she hardly had to check. It was the same time she woke up every morning since her mother had moved in almost a year ago. The alarm was set for 6 a.m., but the days of "sleeping in" till the alarm went off were long gone and seemed like a dream.

The nightly ritual was to wake up at 3:00 and do mental acrobatics. First, she would review her to-do list from the day before. There were always three or four things she had not gotten around to—and many of the things she had gotten "done" were not done as well as they should have been. So she spent a little time critiquing her performance for that. Next, it was time to go over the to-do list for the coming day. This list was always humungous, of course, because of the carryover of things she had not gotten around to the day before. Time and energy were in short supply.

All that was exhausting enough, so it didn't help that she had trouble falling asleep each night. She tried to be in bed around 10 p.m., but it usually ended up being closer to 11:00 or midnight by the time she shut off the night light.

Would that shutting off her racing thoughts were so easy. She had counted enough sheep to clothe the state in wool, but her thoughts would ramble on. It was hard to believe that she used to fall asleep most night before closing her nightly prayer with *Amen.*

So she lay awake obsessing about Mother's pill case. How could she have forgotten to set up the pills? She must have made a dozen mental notes to remind herself yesterday. And then there was the note in her daily planner. Every time she passed the corner of the kitchen counter she thought about it, but there was the phone to answer and dinner to get on and a hundred other things clamoring for her attention. She had even tried a mnemonic device to help her remember to fill the pill case: *Fill chill PILL or CASE of insomnia.* It was a chant intended to remind her to fill the pill case when her husband Steve reminded her (as he had been doing every night for weeks) to "chill out, sweetheart."

Sara thought she might try refilling the pill case as soon as her mom took the daily allotment of pills each morning…. *Hmm, that might work…. No, it wouldn't because what if Mom forgot she had taken the pills and took a second dose.* That would be one of her famous "let's make things worse trying to make them better" type moments. She had gotten good at that! She would end up spending all day at work worrying about whether Mom had taken too much medicine. And work? Lord knows she hardly needed more distractions there.

*Sara, Sara, Sara,* she thought to herself: *How difficult is it, really, to remember those pills? You take the pills and put them in the case. Two pink, one blue, and one green.*

Yet every night, just as she was finally lapsing into sleep, she would remember the pill case—usually when it was too late. So here she was in the middle of the night—awake if barely conscious. *What to do?* If she got up and went downstairs to fill it now she risked waking both her husband,

Steve, who badly needed his sleep, and her mother, Rose, a light sleeper whose bedroom was just off the kitchen.

*Which was worse,* Sara wondered, *risking waking Mom up or having her find the pill case empty at 5:30 a.m.?*

She decided at last that she would wait it out for another couple of hours. No sense waking up Steve or Mom, and since she was now wide awake the chance of going back to sleep was slim at best. She would just lie awake for a little while and go over her to-do list for tomorrow.

They say no good thoughts come at 3 a.m., but Sara smiled when she recalled something her friend Jan said a few days ago. Jan, the psych major turned armchair psychologist, said, "You know, Sara, I wonder if that pillbox is Freudian?" When Sara said, "I don't know *who* makes it?" Jan said: "Freudian, as in *Sigmund Freud.* Could it be your way of saying that your mom's getting older is a bitter pill to swallow?"

Sara thought it was clever. As she lay awake in the silent darkness she wondered if Jan weren't on to something. It *was* a bitter pill, and though she knew very little about Freud she remembered the way the professor in her Psychology 101 class summed up Freud's psychology: *The tighter you harness the dog the harder it will bite.*

*Is that what she had been doing?*

That very night after she got home—very late and worn out—and was sifting through the day's mail her mother asked her something—something about Sally and her major at college. Her mother's words always seemed so critical that it left Sara feeling as if she always had to be on the defense. Sara gave her a quick reply to move off of the subject.

Her mother went on into her room, and Steve said, "You really snapped at her."

"That wasn't snapping," she had told him. "People jump to the conclusion that I am being snappy, maybe I'm just feeling overwhelmed." The minute it came out of her mouth she knew he was right, her frustration and feelings of being "overwhelmed" had caused her to snap at the people she loved.

Steve said, in that disarming way of his, "If I didn't know you better, Sara, I would have sworn that you were still angry at your mom for putting your dad in Pemberton."

"What?" she had said, thinking that comment came out of the blue. "No way!"

Steve just shrugged and said, "I'm just asking."

She stopped herself before she responded to think about what Steve had said and with tears forming in her eyes she said, "May be. *Maybe.*"

And he let it go at that. The man had an impeccable sense of timing.

As she thought about it a few hours later in the still of the night, though, against the steady rise and fall of his breathing beside her, she decided that the honest answer was certainly YES. And she was angry not just at her mother...though she probably took the brunt of it. There was enough anger, it seemed, to go around. She was an equal opportunity angry woman. What we call stress, or depression, or anxiety usually boils down to anger. *Thanks again, Jan,* she thought.

The scary thing was—that was so unlike Sara. She was known for having a short fuse, yes, and a temper that burned hot, white hot—and most often in a flambé of biting sarcasm or a verbal tirade—but burned out quickly. If her fuse were short the explosion that followed was short-lived. It would be over as quickly as it had begun.

At least that was they way it always had been. She was not one to seethe or hold a grudge. Maybe it was because the stakes had never been so high. If somebody makes you a promise—say, to meet you somewhere at 7:00—then fails to keep it, you get huffy and puffy and let it go. If somebody makes your dad a promise—oh, say to have and to hold in sickness and in health—and then *reneges* on it.... Different story.

She decided she had been holding a grudge against her mother ever since the night before she signed Dad into Pemberton. Sara protested that there were other options. She and Steve even offered to pay for a 24/7 care provider to take care of Dad at home, but NO: Mother would have none of it. Sara had said, "Mother, how can you bear to do it to him?" And her mother had looked her straight in the eye and said, "Don't *you* lecture *me* about making family a priority."

That was a slap. It found its mark; it left a mark. Sara hardly needed to be told that she was not the stay-at-home-and-bake-cookies mom that her own mother was. She remembered holding her tongue that night, only so as not to get her dad riled up, but she was thinking: *Some of us have a career; a life outside the home, Mother.*

That would have done no good. Her mother would have smiled and said, "I'm proud of you and all you have accomplished, Sara."

Her mother's way used to be, *kill them with kindness.* There was no contest when it came to who was the better mother—Rose or Sara? Sara was guilty as charged when it came to putting her own priorities before her family sometimes. *A lot of times*, in fact. Sara's mother had put her own priorities before her family *exactly one time.*

And maybe it was that exception to the rule that burnt Sara up. Her mother had always promised that she would never put him in a nursing home. It was a vow her parents made to each other, and she made good on it till that final year when he needed her most. Then she found Pemberton, and that was where her father spent his final moments instead of his home.

*Okay*, she thought, *I am still angry.*

She knew that her mother was worn down and out by the demands of providing care for her husband. She knew that her father had gotten very mean near the end as the disease did a Jekyll-and-Hyde number on him. It transformed the kindest man on earth into a mean so-and-so with a sharp tongue and a foul mouth. She had never heard her parents so much as exchange a cross word until a few months before Mother put him in Pemberton. Sara couldn't be angry at *him*. *How could she be?* It wasn't his fault. He was the victim—well, the main victim. She could hardly blame her father for being angry. *Who wouldn't be in that situation?* He couldn't even remember who he was, much less who anyone else was.

When he would throw his tantrums, her mother would fall to pieces, which would only fuel the fire. It *was* scary seeing him like that. In her entire life, Sara had never heard him utter a foul word or even raise his voice. Sara tried to tell her mother that the more she reacted to his mood the worse it would become. *Just calm down and defuse it, Mother.* Then her mother would turn on her. She was only trying to help, but her mother refused to listen to her advice, and all of her efforts to be supportive fell flat. Her mother simply could not *not* respond to him.

It was excruciating to go visit him and say, "Hi, Daddy," only to have him glance at her and say, "Who are *you*? Who let *you* in here?" It was like being stabbed in the heart every time.

As time wore on, she would go to Pemberton just to keep her mother company. But her mother was a changed person after she put her husband in the nursing home—much quieter, sullen, even indifferent. She had always been bubbly when Sara was around. She was what Sara's father called a "big-time small-talker," but there were times when she wouldn't even talk to Sara during the visit. She would just sit there at her husband's bedside holding his hand, oblivious to everything else.

Sara tried, but after a while she couldn't find a reason to keep forcing herself to go to Pemberton; it wasn't as if she were going to visit her dad and mom. Dad and Mom were both gone; in their place was a father who did not even know who she was and a mother who was lost in his disease. And it didn't help matters that her mother, who hadn't a word to spare her, would become a regular Chatty Cathy when this or that staff member walked in. *So you've not been struck mute after all,* Sara would think; *it's just a case of selective muteness.*

Mother would smile at the nurse, chit-chat with the nursing aid, and thank the food server for all his help. This from a woman who rarely thanked her daughter Sara for anything. She never asked about her grandchildren—Sally and Tommy—but she seemed to know everything about the staff members...how many children they had, what they had done on their day off, and why they got into the nursing field.

As if all that wasn't infuriating—hurtful—enough.... Yes, it was true what her parents had always said about Sara: *She hid her hurt behind anger.* Even if she would trip and fall, slip on the proverbial banana peel, through no fault of anyone, it was a rush of anger rather than pain that she felt first. When the base of the cheerleading pyramid stumbled and caused her to fall and break her wrist during the halftime show, it was anger rather than the pain in her wrist that she felt first. But, again, it would burn brightly then burn out in a matter of seconds.

Anyway, Mother the Mute became Rambling Rose whenever her oldest daughter, Sara's sister Carol, called from California for her twice-weekly update on "Dad's condition" between her hot rock therapy and her yoga class. Mother would provide Carol with detailed updates on Dad's condition, share what the doctor had said during his last visit, and even brief her on how she was feeling about the situation. After sitting there listening to one such 30-minute call, Sara said, "Mother, why is it that I always have to settle for the *Reader's Digest* condensed version while Carol gets the complete and unabridged version?"

Her mother would get very flustered and begin to cry. "I am doing the best I can, Sara. Please, this is no time for that old sibling rivalry nonsense. I was just updating your sister. She lives 2,000 miles away and doesn't have the option of being here every day like you and I do."

"*Option?*" Sara said. "She doesn't have the *option?*" Carol had more *options* than any woman on earth! She had married a real estate tycoon and had never worked an honest day in her life. They were jetsetters. Options?

Mother, not content to let it be, said, "You do have the option of being here every day and you choose not to, so why should I have to spoon-feed you information as if you lived in another state?"

*Whatever happened to that sweet woman who was my mom? First, Dad, now Mom.*

For the first time in her whole life, Sara had wished that she lived in another state — or another country. That way she could go to the spa five days a week to *de-stress* and kid herself that her idyllic childhood was still intact. And she could fly in once a year (twice if they happened to have a layover day to spare en route to some exotic vacation spot) and enjoy the ticker tape parade Mom hosted.

Sara had done the best she could to juggle her responsibilities as a career woman, a wife, a mother, a daughter. But nothing she ever did was either enough or right. And apparently it was too much to ask for her mother to simply communicate with her as she did with everyone else. Sara was the one who had always been there for her parents. She included them in her life and in the life of her family. *Carol?* She had deserted them all years ago.

It was Sara's family who kept the house going after Dad got sick. The Chapins — Sara, Steve, Tommy, and sometimes even Sally who was away at college — would sacri-

26

fice their own family time any old Saturday when a broken toilet needed fixing or the lawn needed mowing. Steve and Tommy were on-call anytime.

And after Mom had her fall and, after months of rehab, it was clear that she would not able to return to her own home, it was Sara who offered to take her in. Even though doing so meant that her whole life was turned upside-down—just when she and Steve were primed for the golden years as empty-nesters. For her part, Carol just went on living her charmed life without even giving a moment's consideration to what it all meant to Sara—except when she called to share some big-sisterly advice on one issue or another.

Carol had no idea what it was like to have to make room for Mom—not just in their house but in their whole family system—to accommodate her needs. Carol's understanding of their mother at 80 was based on the three or four days of "vacation" time she spent out in California with them a couple times a year. And *that* was when mother was still independent and could do everything for herself, not as she was now—needing to have nearly everything done for her.

Funny how big-sister Carol had never once suggested moving their mother into *her* home. Perish the thought that she might have to inconvenience herself to hire a team of full-time caregivers to tend to Mom in a "wing" of their house. Of course, mother would never have moved to California anyway. It would have been like moving into a dorm of strangers, for she hardly even knew Carol's children. She had spent every birthday, baptism, graduation, opening night, home game, and Sunday evening with Sara's children for the past 20 years—all their lives.

When the time had come to make the decision—*what to do about Mom?*—Sara and Steve decided that moving her into their home was the right thing to do. They wanted to keep her close to her friends (the few who were still alive), her church, and (most importantly) her doctors.

Of all the painful tasks that entailed, Sara decided that selling the family home was the most painful. Her parents had lived in that cozy little Cape Cod at 117 Mitchell Place more than 50 years. A lifetime. Sara grew up in that home, and every happy memory in her life was associated with that little house. A year had passed since it sold, and until the previous month Sara drove past the house a few times a month just for old-times' sake. The last time she went by, about a month ago, a crew of landscapers was rototilling the garden, every last flower and shrub that her parents had tended all those years. Sara pulled up to the curb and watched as they destroyed the flower beds that had given such color to her childhood. She drove away slowly, knowing that would be the last time she visited 117 Mitchell.

It was strange to think how that paralleled the loss of her father and, to a less extent, her mother. First, she had lost all that was inside the house. Her mother had saved every crayoned stick drawing from their Kindergarten years and every memento before or since. So when it came time to move her out of 117 Mitchell, they had to part with 50 years of sentimental treasures they had no place to store, along with the furniture and random knick-knacks that would not fit into the one room they had modified for Rose.

It was a heartbreaking ordeal, but Sara had been determined to be strong and keep the "estate sale" as business-like as possible. She couldn't afford to let her emotions get the best of her. There was too much to do. Sara and Steve had to go through every box, cupboard, and closet and help Mom make decisions on what she was going to keep and what would be sold. The last thing any of them—especially her mother—needed was for Sara to fall to pieces. That was the kind of thing they expected of Carol.

And Carol didn't disappoint. She and her husband Bill flew in from Santa Barbara on a breeze of sentimentality the Friday night before the sale was to begin. Of course, they couldn't have come earlier and be bothered with such menial tasks as inventory and pricing. *Mom had Sara and Steve to do that stuff.* Carol, who hadn't darkened the door of the house in a year, was all a mess of tears as she browsed through the items marked for sale. "Oh Mom, you can't part with that," she would say, then: "I'll take this thing—what is this? Oh, we'll have that shipped back home…. You're not asking nearly enough for this…. I'm sure Sara will find a place for that…. That price seems a little high." She appointed herself maven of the moment and dispensed advice freely, which was a good thing, Sara thought, because no one would have paid for it. Carol encouraged Rose to keep everything she wanted to keep, without regard for the fact that Sara and Steve's house was of normal size, not a palatial estate like Carol and Bill's. So it fell to Sara to play the heavy, to have to say, "Mother, we don't have room for this."

Then Carol would say, "Looks like there's no room at the inn." And then the bright idea hit her: "Why don't you and Steve buy the house?"

Sara saw her mother's face light up.

"I thought you and Bill were the real estate tycoons," Sara said.

"But we're way out west, and you two are right here." She went on to say how busy their life was already…and it wasn't an "option they could pursue." Blah. Blah… *Blah.*

*What about Sara's life?* She had a demanding career and a husband and a kid still at home and one in college and (as if that wasn't enough) she was the one tasked with taking care of Mom. It never occurred to her that there was any other *option* besides taking care of Mom. She would never "put" her mother in a nursing home. It was only right that Mom should be with family, and Sara was the only family she *really* had.

*What about the things she and Steve wanted to "pursue"?* Over the years they had often talked (usually in the midst of a bad snow or ice storm) about moving somewhere warmer. They had even gone so far as to investigate the job and housing markets in Arizona and Florida. But then they would wake up from the dream to a life full of responsibilities—and reality—and wait till the next arctic blast to think about the tropics again. Then Dad got sick and they knew that they needed to stay around to care for Mom.

On and on the nonsense went. Sara, still determined to be the strong one, stood there biting her tongue and tapping her foot thinking, "Oh brother," as Carol vetoed the sale of this item or quibbled over the price of that item and ended up shuffling the "keep" and "sell" piles they had spent the week—a very sad week—sorting.

Sara suggested that Carol and Bill take Rose to the town's Spring Festival so she wouldn't have to be there for the sale, but Mom said, "I'm not dead yet. Your father and I worked hard to make a good life for our family. This is my life that is being sold off piece-by-piece, and I am going to be here to see it—to see who buys my life."

In the end they actually ended up donating most of the bigger items and some of the smaller ones to the Salvation Army.

It was heartbreaking.

So Sara had lost the inside of the house, just as she had lost her father to the deterioration of Alzheimer's. His personality, his heart, his mind, were gone. She who had been his princess, his delight, was in the end but a stranger to him. And all that was left was the body in which his soul had once lived. So even near the end she visited him occasionally—because at least she was able to see something of her father.

On her last trip to 117 Mitchell, she knew that all that house represented—its personality and heart—was gone. The ruination of the garden proved that. What was left of her childhood there was alive only in her mind and memories — just as her father was.

But, oh, she did have memories. It seemed that only yesterday she was sitting on Daddy's lap as he read bedtime stories to her and Carol. Unlike other children who dreaded bedtime, she and Carol would race to their rooms and put on their "jammies" and then race back to the family room and climb up onto the couch and take their positions on the left and right side of Dad. There was always enough of him for both of them. He would pull the girls close, and Mom would hand him the "Good Book," and he would read and embellish the stories about Moses, Jonah, and David. Then he would close the Bible and say, "Now how about you girls tell me what you think that story was really all about...."

Without fail...the point he would make is that they, a couple of ordinary but beautiful, bright, and glorious girls from Anytown, USA, had been chosen by God for greatness.

He taught them so many life-lessons. Of the two girls, Sara provided the bigger challenge for their father. She was smart, outgoing, and always up for an adventure. Her spirited personality got her in quite a bit of trouble over the years. She soared high and on occasion fell hard. But even when she got into trouble for some mischief — maybe talking back or violating her curfew — Dad was stern in a loving way, always trying to help her learn a lesson. He was quick to tell her that failure wasn't a bad thing but an opportunity to choose differently next time.

And then there was her mom. Sara had always enjoyed a very close bond with her mother. Whoever said "You can't be your children's friend" had never met Rose Barnes. She was Mom and friend, and Sara could tell her just about anything without fearing being judged or criticized. She could always count on being listened to and loved.

She smiled when she recalled how her mother reacted to the news that Sara had met Steve. Sara met Steve the first day of her freshman year in college in a chemistry class. She called her mom the minute she got back to her dorm room to tell her all about him. "Mom, I just met the man I am going to marry."

Her mom said, "Oh, dear, I'll get my dress to the cleaners and dust off your daddy. Does the young man know about it yet?" They both laughed about how fitting it was the two had met in chemistry class. Then her mother got serious: "Always remember that love is God's gift to us, so just enjoy all that your heart is feeling...and bring him home as soon as you can so Dad and I can meet our future son-in-law."

Her mother had always been so positive. Instead of giving her all the standard parental jazz about how she was *too young* to know what love was and how foolhardy "love at first sight was," she gave her daughter permission to fall in love.

Jack and Rose Barnes were not perfect parents, but they came closer than any other parents Sara had ever known. Some of her friends—and even her own children—went through that teenage phase when they wouldn't even acknowledge their parents. Not Sara. She always wanted them involved in her life. Their little home at 117 Mitchell Place was something of a neighborhood hangout for Sara's friends, who preferred the Barnes' house to their own. They would come in and say, "Hi, Mom and Dad," to Rose and Jack en route to the refrigerator to help themselves to a snack. Mom would say, "The fresh cookies are in the red cookie jar; they might still be warm."

And time and age didn't change any of that. Her parents were invited to her friends' weddings and baby showers and baptisms. It was amazing how her mother managed to keep track of the birthdays and anniversaries of her friends—long before the days of Outlook calendars and PalmPilots—and always made sure to send out a card with a personal note.

*You were blessed with a wonderful father and a wonderful mother.*

Her friend Jan, who referred to Jack and Rose as "Mom and Dad" always said that they were her "happy" parents and would often just shake her head and said, *How lucky can one girl get?*

But all that was past. Just a memory—a sweet memory made bitter by the present reality: Dad was dead and gone, and Mom was just...*gone.*

*If only Mom hadn't been so good and easy all those years it wouldn't be so bad and hard now—now that she couldn't seem to do anything right as far as her mother was concerned.*

It was now 4:30 and the first light of day was turning the room from black to gray. *I am angry,* she thought. *I have become an angry woman—and bitter, too.* Mom was an easy target for all the anger and bitterness. *And Carol?* Being angry at her was nothing new. She had been angry at Carol since the day her big sister left for college and never came back. *Maybe I am mad at myself, too. We didn't exactly take Daddy in, either. And at God—for making my father suffer from that horrible disease that took him away from us twice—first we lost him in mind and spirit and then in flesh. Then there is some resentment for Mom's not being able to control things and allowing them to turn out this way.*

These thoughts startled Sara. What a ridiculous thought— as if her mother could have actually controlled a disease that turned her husband into a complete stranger.

Things had certainly not turned out as she had dreamed. Just when Mom was doing so well and their relationship was nearly back to normal and the empty nest was less than a year away and their careers were on track...Mom fell and broke her hip. And no, Carol, there was no *option* but to take her in, no *option* to move to Phoenix or West Palm Beach.

They couldn't uproot Mom and move her 1,000 miles away from everything she knew, had ever known. Just the thought of having to find new doctors and a new visiting caregiver made Sara's heart race. Mom really liked her caregiver, Lily, who had become practically a member of the family. Lily was a Godsend for Sara, and it was comforting to know that someone was caring for Mom and keeping her company during the day while she and Steve were at work. Sara had interviewed dozens of caregivers before finding Lily. Not only was Lily great with her mom but, as an added bonus, she cleaned the house and made an effort to do the laundry and other chores that had kind of fallen by the wayside after Mom moved in. With her workload and the added stress of having Mom in the house, the little things that needed to be done had became more difficult for her to keep up with.

*Who am I kidding?* Sara thought. She loved having someone else clean her house. Coming home to a clean house and having her laundry clean, folded, and put away was one of the few things she looked forward to about coming home every evening.

It was now 5 a.m.

*Dear Lord, could you just hit rewind on my life for about two weeks—or five years—and do a do-over?*

She lay there in the gray of the bedroom trying to remember what had awakened her in the first place. It was no use. She thought for a moment about getting out of bed and getting a head start on her day. It seemed like a good idea. She had so much to do. She had a team meeting that day to get organized for. She needed to get to the office early and make copies, meet with the team leads, and put together an icebreaker for the meeting. She thought about the conference room layout and the preparations she had already made. With each item she ticked off the mental checklist, she became more overwhelmed—adding mental insult to emotional injury.

Just as she thought—*time to get up*—her eyes closed and she dozed off. The clock read 5:15 a.m.

Only a second later, it seemed, she woke up to the alarm clock honking like a bull horn in her ear. As her hand slapped the snooze button she remembered what had awaken her— THE PILLS! It was 6 a.m.

Then the anxiety tinged with dread came. She knew her mother would be sitting at the kitchen table seething. She threw on her robe and headed down the stairs. Sure enough, mother was sitting at the kitchen table. Sara headed straight for the open pillbox on the counter.

"There were no pills in my case," her mother said. Her face was red. Sara could tell that she was angry.

"I know, I know, Mother," Sara told her, feeling like a little girl chastened for being naughty. "I forgot."

She felt a flush of anger rising through her exhaustion, but she held her tongue and let her mind run riot with the sarcasm. It's not like they both didn't know that the pills were not there. And it wasn't that Sara woke up this morning and said, "Let's pull a fast one on Mom!" or suspected that some pill thief in the night had broken in and passed over the family jewels just to steal the pills from her mother's case. And it wasn't that her mother presumed that the pill fairy who winged in each night to dispense the pills was derelict in her duty.

As Sara approached the counter she noticed that the pill bottles were sitting on the counter right next to the open case.

*I must be losing my mind. Unless there really is a pill fairy! At some point yesterday I must have taken the pills down from the shelf then got distracted and completely forgot to put them in the case.*

Ever since her father was diagnosed with Alzheimer's and the doctors told her that some of the research had found some possible links to heredity, Sara had been hypersensitive to lapses of memory—however trivial. This one wasn't trivial. She tried desperately to recall when she had taken the pills down and what had distracted her, but for the life of her she couldn't recall it. As she shook the pills out of the bottle, she replayed the previous evening after she got home late from the office. To no avail. She quickly decided that it was too early and she was too tired to even try to figure it out.

*Where is my brain?*

She filled a glass with water and handed it to her mother with her pills. Trying to sound cheery, she said, "Here you *go*," letting her voice rise on the last word.

Mother didn't seem happy at all. Sara knew she had been sitting at the kitchen table for at least an hour-and-a-half just waiting to pounce on her with: "There were no pills in the case."

She had better get going. There was so much to do and she could have gotten so much more done by now if only she had not fallen back to sleep. That hour would have made a big difference. She hurried back upstairs to take her shower. Half way up she heard her mother say, "Are you going to have breakfast?"

She asked Sara that question every day, and each day Sara gave the same response: "No time today, Mom." She obviously had no idea how busy Sara was, how hectic her schedule was. Or maybe she expected Sara to fix breakfast for her. That would be "enabling," which as the doctors always said amounted to "disabling." She needed to encourage her mother to remain as independent as she could for as long as she could. Mother was certainly capable of scrambling herself some eggs or boiling water for Cream of Wheat. Lily took care of lunch.

Lily was a Godsend and a wonderful caregiver. Sara had interviewed what seemed like hundreds of applicants to find someone she felt she could trust with her mother; Lily was the first applicant who actually paid attention to her mother. Sara's only issue with Lily is that she didn't want the liability of taking her mom to the doctors, so Sara still had to take time off of work to take her for her appointments. Steve would offer, but Sara wanted to be there to hear what the doctor said. Sometimes things could get lost in translation between the doctor, Steve, and her mom.

It was as if neither of them listened to one thing the doctor said. Then Sara would have to spend her day playing phone tag with the doctor to find out what really happened at the appointment. She had found a good doctor, a recommendation from the social worker at the hospital. It was no surprise to Sara that the doctor seemed annoyed that she would follow up on every appointment. Going with her mom allowed her to be there when the initial comments were made and ask the doctor the questions that needed to be asked directly while her mom's case was fresh in his mind.

Sara was moving none too fast that morning, and by the time she made it back downstairs it was 7:45. She should have been out the door half an hour ago. Her mother was still sitting at the kitchen table when Sara rushed out to the garage. "Bye," she called out just before the door closed behind her.

Perfect timing. *Perfectly awful.* She made it onto the on-ramp of the expressway just at the peak of the morning rush-hour traffic.

# Chapter Two

# 3 a.m.

*Not again*, Rose thought.

She woke up with a start and slowly turned her head and looked at the alarm clock on the nightstand next to her bed: 3 a.m. The curse of the aged, she thought, was to have the time but not the capacity to get eight hours of sleep. For years she had thought how nice it would be when the demands of life were such as to permit her the leisure of retiring early and sleeping a good eight or nine hours to awake completely refreshed.

Like so many other hopes of her youth—mainly that she and Jack would grow old together and healthy until the end—this one had not worked out.

Her eyes gradually adjusted to the darkness of the room, illuminated only by the dim glow of a nightlight in an outlet near the baseboard by the door to the bathroom on her right. She let her eyes take in the room. Some of the furniture was familiar, but it all seemed out of place—the way things do at 3 a.m. The trouble was they had seemed out of place even before she turned off the bedside light and prayed herself to sleep. She recalled telling her husband Jack that the maple dresser, which was a bit tallish, just didn't look right on that wall opposite the bed. Yet there it stood, the shiny brass knobs staring defiantly back at her like golden eyes in the pale glow of the nightlight.

Then she remembered: *I am not at home. I am at Sara's house.*

And, as it always did, the recollection gave her a little ache in the heart that was not unlike the ache in her hip from the arthritis and other pains where the bones had knitted back together. That one was constant, though. Just then the pain was shooting down her leg, and she rubbed it with a circular scrubbing motion, trying to erase it from her flesh. With so much time on her hands it was no wonder she had gotten so good at identifying her aches. She recalled only a year ago sitting in her Sunday school class thinking, "What in the world am I doing in here with all these old ladies with their rheumatism and murmurings?"

Now, she thought, *I* am an old lady, an old lady who can no longer do for herself....

She looked around the room again at the meager belongings she had brought from the three-bedroom Cape Cod she had lived in for almost 50 years. How difficult it had been to try to figure out which things to bring and which to leave behind.... How do you liquidate the accumulated wealth of a sentimental lifetime—to *sell out* to people for whom they meant nothing? *How do you fit 50 years of stuff into one room? You get rid of just about everything.* Sure, Sara had tried to help as much as she could, but they had very different ideas of what was important for Rose to take with her.

Oh how she had cried the day of the estate sale. An estate sale was something that was supposed to happen to your things *after* you die—but it can come close to tearing your heart out when you're there to see people haggling over what to pay for something that, to you, is priceless. Watching all those years of memories sold off for next to nothing had led Rose to lapse into a bout of depression so blue that her internist, Dr. Gordon, had prescribed anti-depressants for her. As if a pill could kill the pain of watching your life auctioned off to complete strangers as you sit by with no power to stop it.

*Well,* she thought, *what choice did I have but to move in with Sara and Steve? It's not like I had a lot of options. The Lord hadn't been ready for me...and they were, or so it had seemed.*

Lord knew they did their best to try to make her comfortable in their home, but after all those months it still just didn't feel like home—and at last she had gotten used to the fact that it never would. For the simple reason that it was *not* her home; it was theirs.

She continued to rub her leg until the shooting pain became a dull ache like the rest of her body. Who would ever have thought that tripping over a throw rug in the bathroom could be the downfall of her whole life? One day she was independent, driving herself around, playing cards with the younger women in the church (because they were "more her speed") a couple of times a week, going shopping and on the bi-annual trips with her friends to Las Vegas. Oh boy, was she ever having fun. Now a 10-minute ride to the doctor's office a few minutes from Sara's house made her feel as though she had walked to Vegas and back.

She rolled onto her side and sat up in the bed and turned on the lamp on the nightstand. She studied the picture of her and Jack. What a handsome man he was, her Jack. When they first met at that USO dance, he came right over and asked her to dance—and dance they did for the next 55 years. He had aged so well, still handsome until the end. The *bitter* end—when Alzheimer's stole him, very slowly, away.

First, it was just forgetting things here and there. "I'm just having a senior moment," he would quip, and they would share a laugh and she would recite Browning's poem, "Grow old along with me! The best is yet to be, the last of life, for which the first was made." He would wink at her and say, "I don't guess a young man would do you too much good at this point anyway, my lady."

Then came that fateful day in September when everything changed. Jack had gone to Dr. Geller's office for a dental checkup and nearly an hour after she expected him back the phone rang. It was a policeman calling to inform her that he had come across Jack sitting by the car on the shoulder of the road some 30 miles from home quite confused.

And in that moment everything changed.

Knowing how things turned out, Rose sometimes wondered whether it would have been easier to accept the news that Jack had been killed in an automobile accident that chilly Autumn day, which is the first thing she thought when she heard the policeman say, "Mrs. Barnes, this is Sergeant Perry with the city police...."

Whoever said *hindsight is 20-20 got it all wrong*. Hindsight is not sight at all. You can no more *see* life in reverse than you can *live* it in reverse, she thought: *So quit wondering about that*.

"Oh, Jack," she whispered, "I miss you, dear."

She held the picture in her hands and steadied it. *My, my, I guess I am getting old*, she thought, recalling her own grandmother's trembling hand when she would read a story to young Rose. She studied the picture of Jack and her that was taken on their 50th wedding anniversary. They had just danced to *Let Me Call You Sweetheart*, one of their favorite songs in the early years of their marriage. They had no idea then how it all would end, how bittersweet their last years together—on earth—would be.

The diagnosis ALZHEIMER's was unbelievable. And Rose didn't believe it till it became impossible not to believe it. They had cried and prayed and consulted every doctor within 300 miles. They tried every medication on earth. Some of them even brought temporary relief for this symptom or that, but there was no wonder drug, no miracle cure, for Alzheimer's disease. They even went to counseling to help them work through their feelings about the diagnosis. With the progression of the disease, however, Rose was left to walk the final miles alone. She worked through the stages of grief, and denial soon gave way to bargaining and then to anger. How angry she was when Jack forgot everything and everyone, including at last who she was. He would call her name in the day and in the night, but when she came he would look at her as if he had never met her and say, "You're not my Rose. I want my Rose."

*I'm still your Rose, Jack,* she thought. Then came a pang of guilt that was more excruciating than all of her other aches and pains put together. "I'm sorry," she whispered. When it became clear that Jack needed more care than she and a home healthcare aide could provide, she was left with no choice — she still found that hard to believe — but to have Jack put in a nursing home. She had always promised him that she would take care of him — in *sickness* and in health. But he was so confused, so combative in his temper outbursts, that she just couldn't take it anymore.

The counselor worked with Rose to accept that she just wasn't able physically or emotionally to handle all of Jack's care needs. She had said, "Rose, it's time to accept the fact that Jack needs more care than you can give. It's taking a toll on you physically now that he needs more help with bathing and dressing. There are a lot of nice places that give good care. That will allow you to spend whatever time is left with Jack being his wife instead of his primary caregiver."

*Easy for a pert young woman of 30 — younger than my Carol and Sara — to say. A disease like Alzheimer's,* she thought, *might just make liars of us all.*

No good thoughts come at 3 a.m., she had always said, and how true it was. A floodgate opened every night about then and Rose guessed she was doomed to relive the whole sad end of her and Jack's romance again and again. *What hell beyond the grave could be worse?* Heaven would be when that nightly replay ended. When there was no remembrance of those final years. They would pick up where they left off with Jack's saying, as he walked out the door that Autumn day for his dental appointment, "When I get back from the dentist's, let's you and me go for some Italian."

He had been gone for almost four years. *Could it really be that long?* Her cheeks were damp and her heart was aching. When at last Jack died it was like losing him a second time. She lost him first to the disease and then to death. She had cared for him at home for three years—first by herself, then with the help of a home health aide—before "putting him" in Pemberton.She hated the phrase "putting him at Pemberton", she didn't "put" him there, she found a place with staff that was trained to meet his growing physical and psychological needs and was awake 24 hours a day to be able to meet his needs.She was too weak to physically take care of him and emotionally it had become too difficult on her every minute of every day.She might have been able to hold out a while longer but, with the doctor and his staff encouraging her to make the difficult choice, she finally relented. Yes, those three years took a heavy toll on her. Looking back, though, she concluded that it was easier in some ways having him home than at "the home." She had spent just about every waking moment with him in the nursing home. Her whole life was organized around getting up in the morning and getting to Pemberton for 8 a.m. breakfast and staying until 8:30 or 9:00 in the evening. How hard it was to leave those first few nights and go home to their empty house.An empty bed.

She hadn't slept a night without him since they were married. Every night for 53 years. Even when the girls were born Jack slept in a chair in her hospital room just to be close to her. When the nurses tried to make him go home he just shook his head and smiled: "If my girls are here, I am here. This man's heart and home is where his girls are."

So they finally gave up and let him camp out in that wiry old chair. One of the nurses even said, "Honey, we should all be so lucky as to have a husband like that." *Blessed, not lucky*—that's what Rose told her.

And if she were to count her blessings, well, how many people could say they enjoyed a blessing every day of their lives for more than 50 years? Only yesterday it seemed she and Jack were young and in love, and now here she was, old and alone in a room in a house that wasn't her own.

She recalled the day Jack came home to their tiny efficiency apartment and swept her out the door on his elbow. "Have I got a surprise for you, my dear!" He held the door as she swung her legs into the black Studebaker and made her promise to keep her eyes closed until he told her to open them. Twice he caught her cheating and pulled off on the shoulder of the road and waited for her to fashion a blindfold out of a handkerchief and fit it over her eyes.

Ten eternally long minutes passed before she felt the car slow to a stop. "Not yet, Rose," he said, as he raced around to her side and helped her out. He removed the blindfold and said, "Now you just keep those baby blues closed until I tell you otherwise, got it?" He steered her by the arm up a few steps, then said: "All right. Open 'em!"

And there it was.

That little Cape Cod that would be their castle for more than half a century. Rose had never seen a more beautiful house—nay, *home*—in her life.

"It's all ours," he announced, with his chest out and his head back. "It's time to move forward with our life and our family," he said, nodding toward her belly. Not that the cramped little apartment they lived in above his uncle's hardware store was so bad; though she would have lived in a straw hut as long as she was with Jack. But it did put her in mind of a Humphrey Bogart movie, with the light from the store's sign pulsing through their bedroom window all night long.

But this.... *This* was a dream home to her. Not one for dramatics, Rose did feel as though she might swoon standing there looking up at the white clapboard trimmed with black shutters, set back a little ways from the gently curving street of the tiny subdivision full of other young families. Jack took her hand and led her up the steps onto the front porch and through the side-lit colonial front door beneath a transom. A narrow driveway canopied by a young pine tree was on the right side of the house and led to a garage tucked away in the backyard.

Over the years they had made that three-bedroom Cape Cod at 117 Mitchell Place their home in every conceivable way. They planted flowers. Lots and lots of beautiful flowers with long stems and bright, cheery blooms in every conceivable hue and smaller ones with tight yellow petals and border beds in reds and blues and golds. Jack planted two *rose* bushes in her honor, one on each side of the front porch stairs.

As their family and belongings grew, they added a large family room off the back of the house and poured a concrete patio between it and the driveway for entertaining. Jack was revered as King of the Grill in the neighborhood, and the neighbors were always welcome when they smelled charcoal smoke wafting on the breeze.

What really made that house a home, though, was sharing the raising of their two daughters—Carol and Sara—with Jack. Carol and Sara were two peas in a pod when it came to Daddy's affection. They were Jack's little princesses. She might have been a little jealous at first, when it seemed that Jack had left his Rose—his first love—for the girls, but Jack's heart was big enough for all of them. They were his girls; Rose was his lady.

Jack helped his daughters plant two dogwood saplings, one for each of them, in the backyard and on every birthday each girl would go out and measure herself against her tree to see which one had grown the most. Rose thought it was funny how people nowadays refer to the 1950s sitcoms such as *Father Knows Best* as a fiction. The Barnes were living proof that that kind of life was no fiction at all. They had lived it...only they hadn't all lived *happily ever after*. But *happily 50 years after* was not so bad at all.

They weren't rich—far from it. But they did have their piece of the American Dream Pie. And they made sure to take a vacation each year to a different historical site. Jack loved to drive—and sing while he drove—and would venture far off course if he saw a sign advertising one type of "wonder" or another (as he called them), a wonder being anything that piqued his interest or tickled his natural curiosity. Once they even veered 300 miles off-course to see the world's biggest ball of yarn. Jack was keen on making the annual trip both an adventure and an educational experience. No mere fun-in-the-sun trips for the Barnes family unless there was some educational value to be found (for instance, that trip they made to an island to watch the nesting of the great logger-head sea turtles).

Jack used to say, "Blonde or no, my girls won't grow up to be dummies. They will experience history—and maybe one day *make* it, not just read about it." The girls were all for it. They loved those family adventures, singing songs in the car, playing games, telling jokes. Those were the best of times.

Jack worked hard and never complained about it. He loved providing for his family. He quickly worked his way up the corporate ladder at the insurance company. So he raised quite a ruckus amongst his corporate partners when he refused to be promoted into any position that would prevent him from coming home every night at a reasonable hour and being with his family on weekends. God and family were always Jack's priorities. Sundays were set aside for church and being together (and Sunday evenings for family Bible study and devotional time), and weeknights and Saturdays were for family—not for the company. He gave himself to the company for 45 hours a week. And they had a good man.

"If you don't have God, kiddos," Jack would say to the girls before he tucked them in each night, "you don't really have anything."

Once the girls were both in school, Rose very gingerly broached the subject of taking a part-time job as a secretary. The last thing she wanted to do was hurt Jack's pride or insinuate that he was not a good provider (he was a *wonderful* provider). She just wanted to find something productive to do with all that time she found on her hands. She suspected that he would be reluctant to agree to it, and at first he was. But she told him that she and the girls found it awkward having to ask him for money to buy him birthday and Father's Day presents. He raised and eyebrow in that way of his meant to say, "You can do better than that." So she told him the truth—that she wanted to get out and do something productive outside the home—and vowed that her part-time work would not take time from the family.

Jack said, "Why didn't you just say that, my dear Rose?"

Rose found a job as a clerk in a distribution center for a large international company in the housewares industry. She loved working outside the home. Raising the girls and making the home was fulfilling, but working at her very own job gave her a sense of independence, and she was delighted at being able to help with an occasional bill or surprise the girls and Jack with little gifts from time to time. And the work itself was exciting. The company had offices all over the world, and Rose got to interact with people of different ethnic and cultural backgrounds. Jack would ask her every evening, "So, what country did you visit today?"

She would tell them all about the people she talked to in other countries and what she was learning about their cultures, and Jack would give her a kiss and say, "Look at my dear Rose, touching lives all over the world." Jack always encouraged her and was genuinely interested in what she was doing. He often told her how proud he was of her—and Jack was a man of his word, so she knew that it was true.

Rose touched their 50th anniversary picture against her breast, then set it, very carefully, back on the table. She couldn't recall the last time anyone had shown any interest in her day.

*You've come a long way, baby,* she thought. *Or have you?* She was 50 years removed from that tiny apartment above Uncle Harvey's hardware store with that bright sign pulsing through the bedroom window all night. But those little nightlights they tacked above the baseboard to keep her from falling in the middle of the night were, if anything, even more aggravating. They had old-folk-proofed the house.

All that was good was past: the precious familiar Cape Cod, the flower blooms in the yard, the dogwood trees to be measured, the love of her life. The glow of those lights on the maple bedroom suite punctuated just how small her world had become.

She looked at the clock again: 4:30. *Might as well get up and move around; helps the legs feel a little better. And there's no sense wallowing in my self-pity.* She got out of bed and put on her robe and slippers and headed out to the kitchen. *Her* bedroom used to be a den, but Sara and Steve turned it into a nice-sized bedroom and even added a full bathroom so that she wouldn't have to negotiate any steps on her way to the bathroom. *Thank God for that kindness.* It was humiliating for her to have to wait for someone to come home to help her up the stairs to take a shower then sit just outside to help her back down when she was done (or keep an ear out in case she took a spill off the shower chair). There was nothing like not being able to get yourself to the bathroom to make you feel like an invalid.

Rose had always showered first thing in the morning. If she slept late, she would have to sit there all day feeling unclean (and hoping nobody would stop by for a surprise visit). That, or she could risk life and limb by climbing up the stairs. She had tried that once, and it ended up taking her over an hour to scale the 13 steps. She recalled how Jack used to quip—from about age 50 on—"Well, it's too late now to die young."

She smiled as she made her way out to the kitchen. In the night light of the microwave oven she felt along the counter for her pill case. She usually took them at 6 a.m., but what difference would an hour and a half make? She picked up the case and jiggled it a little but heard no telltale rattle of pills. *So many pills you'd think I had a drug problem.*

Then one of those little moments of disorientation came. She tried to recall if she had already taken them. *No, no, no.* She had just gotten out of bed, so how could she have taken them already? Sara must have forgotten to fill the case last night. She had arrived home from the office later than usual and looked all out of sorts and was not very talkative. Sara seemed more irritable lately, and Rose was concerned about her youngest daughter. She had tried to ask if everything was all right, but realized when Sara replied, "Nothing," with a snap in her voice that she should back off. *I never wanted to be a burden to my children, and poor Sara....*

Sara had always been such an outgoing child. She was the life of the party and could light up a dark room just with that radiant smile. She had so many friends—and all of them were her "best" friend when she was with them. They always felt comfortable enough to walk into the Barnes household and shout out to Rose, "Hi Mama Barnes." What a joy it was being everyone's "Mom." That was light years ago. Now Sara's countenance had darkened. *How could the poor girl not feel overwhelmed?* And ever since she was a toddling little girl, Sara would bow up and get a sharp edge about her whenever she felt stressed. Rose had learned that the best thing she could do when this happened was just give Sara some space, and in a day or two she would be back to her old self.

That was hard to do now that she was living in the middle of Sara's house. Sara was irritable much of the time, and her mood was bitter. Rose had begun to wonder if there were nothing she could do to appease—if not *please*—her daughter. Another heartache: They used to be so close. They would talk on the phone almost daily, just to bring each other up-to-date on all the goings-on in their lives. Sara would share news about her life as a corporate executive—a real-live businesswoman; Rose would share information about the mission trip she had taken to Costa Rica or Bolivia or the fabulous Caribbean cruise she had taken.

Now the extent of their conversation was pills, doctors, insurance, and medical issues.

*Well, she shouldn't have to treat me like I'm a little child anyway*, Rose decided. *I'm old enough to get my own pills.* With that in mind, she began trolling through the cupboards—as quietly as she could—trying to recall which one housed the pharmacy of pills she took daily. *I should have bought stock in some pharmaceutical companies.* If only she could take her own pills, well, that would be one less thing Sara would have to worry about. But before she could take them she had to find them.

After her search of the lower cabinets turned up nothing in the way of her "meds," she very slowly slid one of the chairs from the kitchen table over to the counter, being careful not to make too much noise, and climbed up onto it. *If I fall off of this I'll break more than my hip*, she thought.

Steadying herself as best she could she pressed on with the task at hand. She prayed, "God, if you help those who help themselves...please help me now."

In the second upper cabinet she came to, the one above the microwave oven, she discovered the mother lode of meds. She had to work fast—well, as fast as she could. It wouldn't do for Steve or—*Lord forbid*—Sara to bust her in the act of being self-sufficient. She would get a stern talking-to for trying to do something on her own, for herself, for just trying to help. It was ironic how she had lived all of her life (and certainly all of their young lives) taking care of everyone else, and now they spoke to her as if she were a child.

Nobody's fool, Rose had had the good sense and fore-sight to put the dish towel in the sink to muffle the noise of the bottles as she dropped them down one at a time knowing that she would need both hands free to keep herself from pitching off into the floor.

Once down from the chair, she whispered a prayer of thanksgiving. She looked at the pill bottles and wondered why they had to make the writing so small? If they had large-print Bibles, they should have large-print bottles. To treat all-important information with the same level of care and respect.... She tried reading the labels with her glasses on and off, and though in the right light and with just the right tilt of her head she could make out the name and directions she just couldn't make out which ones she took when. She tried to remember whether the pills she had taken every morning for the past two years were pink or blue. *Pink or blue?*

Dr. Gordon was always adjusting her medications—she was, he joked, his favorite guinea pig—when she made her bi-monthly visits. *Pink or blue? Or purple?*

It was no use. It wouldn't do for her to OD on the wrong medications and be found at the last on the kitchen floor in her nightgown. She would simply have to wait for Sara to wake up. Rose put her face in her hands and thought: *I am a burden. Here I am, I can't even figure out what pills I take. So it falls on poor Sara to have to set up my pills, and the poor girl has so much on her plate with her career and her own family to tend to.*

Just then she heard the quick thudding of footfall on the stairs. Rose composed herself as best she could and turned as Sara staggered into the kitchen on heavy feet.

"There were no pills in my case," Rose said feeling the heat rise in her cheeks. *How embarrassing it was being dependent at 80-some years old.* Hearing her own voice echo in the early morning quiet, Rose was painfully aware of how ashamed she must sound.

"I know, I know, Mother," Sara responded, curtly. "I forgot."

*Funny how Mom had given way to Mother....*

*Boy, am I going to be in trouble*, Rose thought, *when she sees those pill bottles on the counter.*

Sara didn't seem to think anything of it. She set the pills and a glass of water on the kitchen table before her and said, "Here you *go*." Her voice was strained; she must be irritated.

Rose made a note of the pills: *Two pinks, one blue, one green.* Though recent experience had taught her that "for future reference" was all but a thing of the past. Unless she wrote something down it would be gone in a matter of minutes. She popped the pills and washed them down with the water but still felt too embarrassed to make eye contact with her daughter.

And just like that the moment passed. Sara turned and headed back up the stairs. Rose called out, "Are you going to have breakfast?" Just once she wished that Sara would take a moment to eat. She would be happy to scramble her some eggs and put on some Cream of Wheat or even pack a light breakfast she could take with her. Rose had always insisted that the girls eat breakfast to get energy to start the day.

"No time today, Mom," Sara called back from halfway up the stairs.

Rose felt relieved that she hadn't been lectured on getting those pills down at peril of life and limb.

Rose considered taking her shower but decided to wait until Sara left for the office. She didn't want to get in the way. Sara sometimes used Rose's bathroom to put her make-up on before leaving.

She put on a pot of coffee thinking: *Wouldn't it have been nice if I had thought to put on the coffee before Sara got up—instead of spending the better part of an hour fooling around trying to find my medicine?*

By the time Sara made it down it was 7:45 and, running late, she had no time for coffee and less for conversation. She was out the door to the garage with a clipped, "Bye."

Sara worked so hard and had done so well, rising to the executive level in the business world and managing to keep her family well-taken care of. Sara had always been a "high achiever." She was voted "Most Likely to Succeed" in her senior year of high school. She was not content to be a stay-at-home mom. That was not "fulfilling enough" for her.

Rose's own boss at Langford Retail Distribution, Mr. Sanders, had on several occasions through the years asked her to come on full-time, but she politely declined him each time with the same line: "Thank you so much, I appreciate the offer, but I already have a *full-time* job," by which they both knew she meant her family. She preferred her time at home. She wouldn't have traded being there with her girls the moment they got off the bus every day for any six-figure salary or fancy title in the world. She treasured those moments listening to them share what was going on with their studies and romantic interests and extracurricular activities. Sara was a cheerleader and Carol was a letter athlete. Rose valued the flexibility her part-time work afforded her.

She was a regular chaperone on field trips and never missed a PTA meeting.

Times had changed. Sara had worked 10- or 12-hour days for years aspiring to the next promotion...and maybe some of it was at the expense of her family. Rose couldn't help but feel a little bit disappointed in Sara. She was even so busy that she stopped coming to visit her father at some point. *She could have at least continued to come to keep me company, to give me a little support.*

*No*, she thought, *it's not for me to judge. How selfish I have become in my old age.*

But judging was one thing and wondering was another. And Rose couldn't help but wonder if Sara hadn't missed out on some things.

It wasn't that she had neglected her children. She was there for all the Big Moments—birthdays, baptisms, graduations, award ceremonies, championship games. It was the Bigger Moments that Rose wondered about—kissing the boo-boos and making them all better, helping Sally through her first crush or Tommy when his classmates were teasing him. The Bigger Moments that come just from taking a few minutes every day after school to reconnect. Those were the precious moments that Rose so cherished when she looked back on her life from the distance of old age.

*Am I being judgmental? Just because Sara has set a different course for herself and her family, does that make her wrong?*

Rose decided that she simply could not relate to Sara's need for promotion—her drive to succeed—outside the home. No one at 80 regrets not spending more time at work. Rose could vouch for that. She thought of the countless promotions Jack had declined because taking them would have *stolen* time from her and the girls.

*Family doesn't mean what it used to. Every commercial on TV was designed to convince families that what they have is not good enough—that it is things, not people, that matter most.*

A few minutes after Sara left, Rose decided the coast was clear for her morning shower. As she stepped into the bathroom (fully functional for any crippled person, which was how she thought of herself now that each passing day left her less capable of doing for herself), she thought: *I really shouldn't be so judgmental; I should consider myself fortunate, if not blessed, that Sara and Steve were able to take me in and even remodeled a living space for me.*

The walk-in shower and bench were a daily reminder of that awful day when her toe caught on the bath rug at her home and sent her tumbling into the side of the bathtub. She had lain there on the floor for hours—naked, cold, and terrified—until she finally managed to drag herself in to the phone to call for help. Then she fought to stay conscious through the pain long enough to cover herself so as to spare the paramedics—not to mention herself—that indignity. How she would have hated for them to tell her family they had found her naked.

After making that call and getting herself into a housecoat she did in fact pass out from the pain and came to only after her friend Mary and the paramedics arrived. A chilling thought came to her: *Just as it might have been easier, if not better, for Jack to have died in a car wreck that day when he got lost, so it might have been easier, if not better, for me to have never come to after taking that fall in the bathroom....*

"The Lord giveth and the Lord taketh away," she reminded herself, as she eased herself onto the special non-slip flooring Steve had put in so that she would not have to, as he put it, "play hopscotch" over small rugs in the bathroom. Such a fine man, Steve, so thoughtful. So much like her own Jack in so many ways.

She sat there and let the hot water wash away the cares of the morning. It's not like she could run a marathon...but boy could she do some thinking. *What else was there to do but think?*

She reached for the soap but the dish was empty and then she remembered: Sara set the new bar of soap on the vanity. When she turned to swing herself around to put herself in position to reach out and get the soap, that telltale pain in her right hip shot up and down the whole right side of her body. "Ow," she said, and almost immediately there came a knock on the door.

"Rose, you okay?" It was Steve.

Rose winced and tried to compose herself before answering. "I'm okay, Steve," she said, but even she could hear the strain in her voice.

"Is there anything I can do for you, Rose?" he asked, and she could tell by the rising volume of his voice that he had pushed the door open just a little.

Her first thought was, *Do you have a gun?*

She would certainly rather die than have her favorite son-in-law have to see her in this state. "I'm fine, dear," she told him. The pain had eased up a bit. "I'm actually having one of my lucid moments; I forgot to bring the soap into the shower with me."

"Ah, I see it," he said. "I'll just slip it around the curtain to you. Don't you worry, I won't look. I'm a happily-married man. I promise I won't even sneak a peak."

Steve was a master when it came to using his charming sense of humor to defeat the awkwardness of a moment such as this.

She couldn't help but chuckle. "See that you don't," she told him. "I'm afraid it might kill you."

Rose smiled—really smiled—for the first time in days. Sara was blessed with Steve, just as Rose herself had been blessed with Jack. She and Jack had both liked Steve from day one and had only grown fonder as the years passed. Steve was what her granddaughter Sally (Sara and Steve's daughter) called "a total package." He was handsome, easy-going, bright, witty, and oh how he loved Sara and was not afraid to tell you that she hung not only the moon but the sun and stars, too.

Those two made a handsome couple—both so full of life and fun. Steve was wonderfully supportive of Sara. Through the years he was there to take up any slack (*now that was a terrible choice words*, she thought) created by Sara's grueling work schedule and commitment to her career. He was great with the kids—always coaching this soccer team or that softball team or teaching the youth Sunday school class. And he was so good to Jack up until the very end—and sometimes she suspected that Jack's illness and death aggrieved him more than Sara.

*What a terrible thing even to think.*

It was enough to say that Sara—indeed the whole Barnes family—was blessed to have Steve Chapin. Rose was blessed that his work as an independent computer consultant enabled him to work from home three days out of five. She did her best not to distract him from his work, but she had to admit that she took quite a bit of comfort just in knowing that someone else was in the house. Not to mention that the one-cup conversation in the kitchen each morning before he went off to do his work either at home or at one of his client's sites was usually the highlight of her day.

Today she had physical therapy to look forward to.

# Chapter Three

# 8 a.m.

S ara always tried to use the 35-minute drive in to the office as downtime. She didn't even turn her cell phone on till she got to work. She would tune the stereo to an easy listening station—avoiding the nerve-wracking morning shows—and just relax her mind and try to take the time to stop and *see* the roses (in this case, the October trees in their gorgeous fall colors) for there was nothing to smell but exhaust.

But this morning she was 50 minutes behind schedule and the volume of traffic was building. *No use trying to relax.* Downtime was one thing; *down* time was another. And this morning she was down, as in down in the dumps.

She turned off the radio and scanned her mental checklist of all the things she had to do at work. She had tried making written to-do lists every day, but that became just one more thing to do and so she had resorted to mental checklists. The other reason was that she wanted to keep her mind exercised and sharp—that dread fear of having an Alzheimer's gene again. But recently her mental checklists seemed to be written with invisible ink, and because the tasks weren't written down in all their overwhelming glory most days she forgot something.

She had issued a memo about the all-hands on deck benefits meetings scheduled for 1 p.m. today. The first thing she needed to do was send a follow up e-mail this morning to make sure all managers reminded their staff to attend the mandatory meeting.

The new plan had been six months in the making—six months of grueling 12-hour days. Sara was determined to put together a world-class benefits plan for the employees of Olson Industries. She had left nothing to chance and no detail escaped her attention. She had even made sure there was a provision for caregiver benefits so that the employees could designate a percentage of their pre-tax earnings to fund childcare for their children or adult day care for an elderly family member.

She had never really given much thought to adult day care before her mother moved in. Not that Rose Barnes was keen on the idea of adult day care. Sara had looked into it when she first moved in, but her mother was offended by the suggestion; the whole thing was condescending and childish, she said.

"What am I going to do all day in daycare," her mother had asked, "play bingo? I *hate* bingo! I guess I could go out on the playground and swing. *Weeee.*"

Sara gave her the spiel that the Sunshine Adult Day Care Center offered a host of activities other than bingo. It was a *senior* center not a *child*care center.

Mother said if that was the case then why didn't they call it a senior center instead of a day care center. Okay, so that *was* a good point. Then Sara suggested that she take the senior bus to the senior center. Rose would have none of that. "I'm not going to start riding on the short bus now," she said, "and besides, I'm a too old to make new friends. I guess my days of socializing are over."

Not everyone felt that way about adult day care, of course, so Sara was determined to provide that option to

Olson employees...even if her own mother thought the whole notion ridiculous.

Sara wondered why she was feeling so down—aside from the fact that she was running on three hours of fitful sleep. Then her eye caught the date on the dashboard clock: October 12. It was the anniversary of the day she got the call at work from a social worker who told her that her mother had signed her father up for Hospice Care and wanted to know if there was anything they could do to help her. Sara recalled bluntly responding "I'm sorry. *What* did she sign him up for?" Apparently their staff was trained to respond to this type of question, and so the very soft-spoken woman on the other end of the phone shared with Sara that her father's physician had determined that he was in the final stages of life, meaning he had less than six months to live. Hospice would be providing extra nurses' aides along with a social worker and a pastor to help not only her father but his family as well.

Though she was upset receiving the news from a stranger via phone instead of her mother in person, after speaking with the social worker she felt comforted knowing that her father would have extra nursing visits there at Pemberton. Sara had never heard of hospice before, but she was quickly convinced that it was the most blessed and dignified way for her father's life to end. The hospice staff was specially trained to care for the terminally ill and to handle both the physical and emotional issues involved with the final stage of life. They did their jobs in accordance with the hospice philosophy—to ensure that the dying depart this world with dignity and comfort—and the hospice approach, which was holistic in caring for mind and spirit as well as the body. In her father's case, it was just body and spirit; by then not much was left of his mind.

The hospice nurses were as much a source of comfort to Rose, Sara, and Carol as they were to Jack. They were there at the very end to call the family when it was clear that he had reached his final hours and to help them with those dreaded calls to have his body transported to the funeral home and make arrangements. On that chilly December morning when they called Sara to let her know that it wouldn't be long until her father "passed away," her initial decision was not to go. The hospice nurse was content to respect her wishes, but Steve was not. He said, "Honey, I know how hard this is for you, but I really think you need to be there for your mother."

So in the end she went. The hospice nurse greeted her at the door and explained what she should expect. Her mother was sitting on the bed holding his hand and talking to him very quietly—just above a whisper. Sara stayed back just inside the door so as not to disturb the last words her mother would ever say to her father.

She would always remember her mother's face at the parting, so full of sadness and anguish, and how she was leaning over so close that her lips were almost touching his ear as she said her goodbye, and how tightly she was gripping his hand, as if maybe she could hold on tight enough to go with him to heaven and they wouldn't have to be apart.

Then her mother was talking louder, telling him that it was okay to let go, to be free of his life here on earth, and be with his Savior. She told him that she and his girls would be just fine and that before they all knew it they would be together again. It was in that moment that Sara realized how truly connected her parents were.

She had always known that her parents loved each other. In the age of divorce, when half of her friends' parents opted out for one reason or another, she knew that they would always be together—not just for moral reasons but for emotional reasons, spiritual reasons. They were truly one flesh. And Sara knew till the end that even if Jack Barnes didn't remember anyone else, somehow he remembered his

Rose—maybe not by name, but to him she was his sweet flower and they were connected in soul and spirit.

So it was no surprise that as soon as her mother told him that she loved him and kissed his cheek, he gave a shallow heaving breath and was gone.

Her mother knew he was gone but she sat there holding his hand for another few minutes, gently shaking it and saying, "Happy Birthday, my Jack. Your new life starts today. Hold a place for me."

Sara recalled how, in the latter stages of the disease, her father not only was not himself but he didn't even look like himself. Jack Barnes had always been so full of life. He stood a little over six feet tall and had a full head of thick black hair that aged into a beautiful silver with gentle waves and was the envy of other men his age (and many women). His sharp blue eyes and bright smile could light up a room. He was never seen at work without a three-piece suit on; at home, it was slacks and a golf shirt; at church on Sundays, a dark suit and tie. He was of the mind that it is only right that we wear our best clothes for God and our football jerseys on game days for the Chicago Bears. After church during football season he would immediately change into his Chicago Bears jersey.

As a child Sara had felt so safe in the arms of her gentle giant of a daddy. And ever since she had always known that he "had her back." He had a way of assuring her that everything would be okay, that there was never a thing in the world to worry about. By contrast, the man who lay those many months in the bed at, Pemberton Nursing Home in sweat pants and a t-shirt was frail and thin, wasted away. The skin on his hands was so papery thin that she could see every vein and bone. His immaculate silver hair, once so thick, had thinned and faded to a dull gray.

Sara never saw him walk after he moved into Pemberton. After several weeks of trying to get him up and walking, the staff gave up and assigned him to restorative therapy for daily leg, arm, and body-shifting exercises to keep the blood flowing to his extremities, which they told Sara would keep him from getting those dreaded bed sores from lack of movement.

Sara had watched exactly one such "workout session." Though the aide was competent and very gentle with him, it was simply too painful for Sara to watch a stranger moving her father around like a rag doll. That was the first time it hit her—very hard—the truth that her father was never going to get better.

Then there was the funeral. Hospice was a blessing. They helped mother with all of the arrangements. The mortician did the best he could to make Jack Barnes look, well, *not so dead*. Sara remembered thinking how strange it was to see him lying there dressed in one of his Sunday suits, but true to his wishes her mom thought it was only appropriate that he be in his best suit to meet Jesus.

What was strange was not that he was in a suit—he wouldn't have had it any other way—but that it was so big on him now. They had taken it in as best they could, but he still looked like a child wearing an adult suit. His wedding ring was on, but it was obvious that he hadn't worn it that last year because it was three sizes too big for his ring finger.

Sara had wanted a two-day wake culminating in the funeral, but mother opted instead for a three-hour "viewing" at the church with the funeral immediately following. She said that it was simply more than she could handle having to stand and talk to so many people for hours on end. She wanted the services over quickly so they could lay him to rest.

So much for that. As it turned out, they had to schedule the funeral service on the fourth day after he died because Carol had to make her arrangements to take the kids out of the private school they attended and make travel arrangements in from California.

After the funeral was over and Carol had gone back to California, her mother took something of a vow of silence when it came to that final year of Dad's life. She wanted no part of any conversation that touched on the nursing home, hospice care, or the funeral. It was as if the last few years hadn't happened at all or had merely been some bad dream that they all just woke up from one morning fresh and alive and ready to go on with life as usual.

To make matters worse: Steve would take mother's side, and that—*that*—made Sara nuts!

He would say, "Honey, your father was *her* husband, and let's just respect her decision to either discuss or not discuss that time."

*What about her?* Sara thought. *Her husband was, after all, my father.*

So it was *not* okay for Sara to discuss how stressful it was for her to see him in the nursing home, and how hurt she was that he had forgotten her, and how sad she was that with him went the one person in the whole world who could really relate—her mother. She tried talking to Carol about it a few times, but Carol had been so removed from the day-to-day of what was happening that she couldn't really relate and usually ended up mouthing some platitude.... "Sara, he suffered so much. He's in a better place."

She shared her feelings with Steve, but after a while even he seemed to get tired of hearing her replay in sad detail the last year of his father-in-law's life. Steve suggested that she go talk out some of her issues with a counselor.

*But counselors couldn't possibly understand. They weren't there. It wasn't their family.*

She wanted to talk about it with her family—with those who were supposed to love her and, more importantly, loved her father. Besides, she protested, who had time to go to a counselor?

So she just put the proverbial lid on it and took it underground. Instead of grief and sadness it was easier to feel anger; *back to Freud*. She would have to share this insight with Jan. Sure, she would bring up little things about her dad from time to time, but then she would feel the tears coming, so she stopped herself before she started to cry.

It was on *down time* days like this that she would always pick up the phone and call 117 Mitchell and somehow just hearing her dad's voice settled her when she was anxious and lifted her spirits when she was depressed. Oh how she missed him. He was true north on the compass of her life and he always pointed up—assuring her that God had a plan for her no matter what struggle she was going through. When she lost him, she lost so much, a piece of her heart, and in the end she lost even the comfort of being able to mourn with those she loved.

Rose was a woman on the move after Dad died. She wasn't one for *withering in despair* all alone at 117 Mitchell Place. She would fly out to Santa Barbara and spend a week or two with Carol and Bill. She would take day trips with her friends from the senior center, mission trips with her church, and even a Caribbean cruise! When she *was* at home, she spent most of each day tending her flower beds. Maybe that was *her* therapy. Flowers make good counselors.

If only Sara knew that her mother felt sad or lonely, or scared or angry, or whatever, it would somehow make her feel better. Not that she wanted her mother to feel that way—well, not exactly—but just knowing that she was feeling anything about that horrible year would at least validate Sara's own feelings of loss and...all those other things.

*Anger.*

The traffic was moving then, but she was well over an hour behind. She hit the gas and turned the radio back on and tuned to the Top 40 station, hoping that listening to some mindless chatter from the morning drive team could distract her from her own mind's chatter. It was working. She was actually smiling at some third-grade joke the DJ had told until a guy in a blue land barge SUV cut her off.

She laid on the horn and yelled out the window, "You son of a witch, where did you learn how to drive?! You don't own the road!"

She pounded the steering wheel. She could feel her heart begin to race as she just went on and on, yelling and cursing, never realizing that the blue SUV was already 10 cars ahead and nearing the end of the exit ramp.

*Anger.*

She pulled into the parking deck of her office building with flushed cheeks and damp eyes and a racing heart.

*Another day in paradise.*

# Chapter Four

# 8 a.m.

Rose and Steve ended up having a two-cup conversation that morning. He barely touched his cinnamon bagel, but he had a huge appetite for learning all about Rose and Jack's life back in the period when the girls were going off to college. He wanted the details, and she was happy to share them. She couldn't always remember what happened 30 minutes ago, but she could tell you exactly what she had for dinner 30 years ago (down to the gravy).

Steve remembered that she and Jack had made room in their own "empty nest" for Jack's father Cecil, who came to live with them for three-and-a-half years after Jack's mother died. The girls were in college by then, and so they had plenty of room for him at 117 Mitchell. It required some adjustment, of course—poor Steve and Sara were all too aware of that—but they made room for him. Sara was happy to let him take her room.

"By then," Rose told Steve, "she had met you and didn't think she'd be coming back to *our* home."

Steve grabbed her hand and gave it a shake. "You and Jack did such a wonderful job with the family, Mom." Then he caught sight of the wall clock and said, "Oops. But I'm not going to have a job if I don't get a move on. I'm working at a client's site today."

Then he gave her hand a final, gentle shake and kissed her cheek then grabbed his jacket and hat and rushed out the door at such a pace that he nearly dove into the garage.

*What a dear man he was.* She wished just once she and Sara could have a two-cup conversation (she would gladly settle for a one-cupper, seeing that they exchanged maybe 10 words total on a typical morning). Even on weekends, Sara had no time to spare lollygagging around chatting with her mother.

*I wonder if she would talk to me even if she did have the time?* Rose thought.Lately, she had such an edge about her— a kind of annoyed resentment. And Rose had learned over the months that anything she did to try to make it better only made it worse. *Whoever said "No good deed goes unpunished" had been a fly on the wall on one of those occasions when Rose tried talking to Sara.* Rose had to be the strong one after Jack died. She did her grieving in private and kept her own counsel when it came to her Loss. Lord knew she had plenty of time to do her private grieving.

Steve rushed back in to retrieve his forgotten attaché and ran back out. He and Sara were always running, mostly out the door, leaving her with even more of that "private time." She thought back to when she and Jack were their age. Things weren't as urgent back then. You got up each morning, had a full breakfast, and moseyed out to do whatever the day called you to do.

*Moseying,* she thought: No one really moseys anymore. It is a lost art, moseying. There was nothing slow-paced about people's lives these days. Even Sara's children, now grown and off in college—Sally a junior and Tommy a freshman— were constantly on the go. Sally was on the Dean's List every semester and a standout on the college cheerleading squad, and Tommy was on his college Drama Team and spent his free time working on his 1967 Mustang (that had been the only brand-new car Jack had ever bought) or playing golf. He always told her, "Grandma, how could I ever hope to get ahead in business if I don't play a mean game of golf."

Rose took a sip of her coffee, now lukewarm, and decided to freshen her cup and finish reading the paper. You know you're getting old when you make sure to read the Obituary page every day to see if any of your friends (or enemies) have passed—or to make sure you haven't! That was comforting some days. She got a little kick out of her own joke.

She used to wake up with the sun brightening the room (she had never cared for window shades); now she woke up with the pain radiating from her hip. The morning person had become a middle-of-the-night person. Not that it mattered much what time it was, or whether the sun or the moon was in the sky. She probably couldn't even tell you what day it was if doing so could keep her from tomorrow's Obit page. Every day since she had been at Sara's was about the same.

Most days went something like this: Wake up between 3 and 5 a.m. with a searing pain radiating from her hip throughout her whole body; lie awake and review her 80-some years of life; stumble out of bed and go into the kitchen; take her pills for the day (was it two blues or two pinks...or two greens and...? Never mind); sit at the table in the dark passing some of that "private time," *processing her emotions,* that's what the counselor used to call it; have an awkward encounter with her youngest daughter (so awkward and tense that the only saving grace was that it was brief); share 10 or 15 minutes chatting with Steve over coffee; take a shower; spend some more "private time"; spend a few hours with Lily; spend some more "private time" before Sara and Steve got home; eat dinner, mostly in silence; watch TV, usually alone; take more pills; go to bed.

*Rinse and repeat.*

71

Rose had never been one for sitting around watching TV. Never cared for soap operas or sit-coms. There was always too much to do. She prided herself on keeping the house clean and enjoyed the feeling of accomplishment it gave her. Her garden was her joy. She could *always* find something to do in this flower bed or that. There was a cedar log garden swing out in the backyard, and she and Jack would sit out there drinking fresh-squeezed lemonade most nights from spring till fall enjoying the scents and colors of the beautiful flowers—but mainly enjoying each other. Jack, who knew about a lot of things, knew nothing about the technical names of flowers.

So Rose would say, "What do they call that one over there, Jack?" He would say, "I don't know what *they* call it, but I call it a 'Smiling Yellow.'" She would say, "Perfect." For *Smiling Yellow* was a much better name than *daffodil*.

When Jack moved into the nursing home she would bring fresh flowers from the garden every few days to brighten his room. Sometimes she would come in and find his gaze fixed on the bunch of flowers. The nurses told her that he often craned his neck as if to smell them, and when he did they would bring the vase over and let him take in the scent. He would take in a deep breath and smile.

Once the nurse told her that when she moved the flowers so he could smell them, she said, "Aren't they beautiful daffodils?" and she said that Jack said very clearly, "Those are Smiling Yellows." Rose was both happy and sad to hear it: Happy at the thought that this may have brightened a very dark existence and sad at the thought that deep down he really was still in there but had no way of getting out.

After he passed, gardening became her therapy. She would spend hours on end tending her flowers. Then she would end the day in the swing drinking lemonade. Sometimes she sensed him there with her—unlike now, when he seemed so long gone. Rose wiped a tear from her eye, missing him sorely and acutely aware of how alone she was in Sara's house. Better try to do something—anything—to pass the time until Lily comes.

Lily was a sweet soul. But to be honest Rose didn't always understand what she was saying between Lily's thick accent and Rose's hearing challenges, so their time together consisted largely of Lily's saying something and Rose's smiling and nodding in reply. Lily made Rose lunch, bless her heart, but cooking wasn't her forté. To be polite, Rose would gnaw and nibble until Lily left the room and then she would toss it in the garbage can. After Lily went home Rose would make herself a sandwich.

*Better remember to fix a snack before Lily gets here so I will have enough energy to get through the day —especially in case Lily fixed one of those really "exotic" old country dishes for lunch.*

She drained the last of her coffee, which by now had turned cold, then got up and placed her cup in the sink. She rinsed the other cups and placed them in the dishwasher. What a marvelous invention the dishwasher was, especially to some old woman whose once nimble fingers were gnarled by age and arthritis.

Used to be she was quite the note-writer. She would handwrite notes to her friends and send them off so that, if nothing else, they would have something in the mailbox besides bills. Now she could barely write her own name in a hand that she could read. Another loss. Old age was a time of Loss. It had started off with the big losses: Jack, her independence, her home and garden, her relationship with her youngest—and closest—daughter, and was now a series of smaller losses, one or two a week, that left her feeling Lost.

After loading the dishwasher, she stood at the sink for a moment, confused. *Wasn't there something she was supposed to do today?* She used to have her calendar down pat. But that was when she "had a life," as they say. Lunch with friends, bridge games, trips with the senior center or with the church missions ministry. *Why would I need a calendar now? To X off the days like a prisoner...until I'm set free.*

*Was it a doctor's appointment?* No, she had just gone last week to see Dr. Gordon...or was it the bone doctor, Dr. Porter, no: Peterson. *Oh, what did it matter anyway?* Still there was something nagging at her. What day is it? Monday or Tuesday. Thursday? *It is October.* She knew that. At least she knew that.

She went to the living room, thinking that maybe something on TV would jar her memory, and looked at the four remote control devices on the end table. People used to have to get up to change the TV. She picked them up, one at a time, and pointed it towards the TV and started pressing buttons. They were small and hard on an old woman.

Not the first one.

Nor the second one.

*Aha!* The third one turned it on.

For a moment she wondered why she had even turned the TV on. Times like these made her suspect that she might be losing her mind. Wandering in and out of rooms, not remembering why she was there.

She was brought back to the living room of Sara's home by the sound of the TV announcer saying, "That's all for this Tuesday morning, October 12."

Of course, she thought, it's physical therapy day. Every Tuesday and Thursday she went for her therapy. Oh how she hated going to therapy.

She always went in feeling merely bad and came out feeling horrible, the pain in her leg all stirred up and bone-weary from the workout. It took her about a day to recover, and then back she went. She went not for herself but for Sara, who was still clinging to the belief that her mother would be able to do for herself again—and get out of her house. Today she really didn't want to go. She had woken up in pain and the therapy would make it worse: Therapy is for those who can get better.

Nearly a year had passed since her fall. Two weeks in the hospital followed by months in Pemberton for rehabilitation. She had insisted on going to the home where Jack had been. She knew the staff there and had spent so much time with them that it was almost like home. Sara wanted her to go to another facility—one closer to her house. She also thought it would be too difficult for her mother to be at the home where Jack had lived…and died.

Rose knew it was really Sara who didn't feel comfortable going back there. She could hardly bring herself to come visit her father during the last six months of his life because, she said, it was too hard for her to see her father like that. Rose could feel herself becoming a little steamed at that though that it was too hard *for Sara*, as if his disease had been all about her.

What about her poor father having to spend his final days confused and in need of help with every facet of life, surrounded by strangers, including Rose? How frightening that must have been for him. The least those who loved him—his wife and daughters—could do was go and visit him…especially since something as small as flowers from the garden seemed to bring him some joy. How much more seeing his daughters could have brought him!

She expected that kind of thing of free-spirited Carol, but not of Sara…. Sara was the one who could be counted on to take care of problems. She was the responsible one. *Wasn't it supposed to be the other way around? Weren't oldest children supposed to be the responsible ones?*

Sara was very helpful when Rose needed to find a nursing home for Jack—even though she could hardly stand the place. And it was Sara who stayed on top of the doctors and staff when Rose was in the hospital and rehab and who took her in when it was clear that she could not return home to independent living at 117 Mitchell.

Carol and Sara were so different, in just about every way, yet for some reason they had always felt the need to compete with each other. At times, Rose felt caught in the middle. It didn't help that Carol was free with advice for such a free-spirited, live-and-let-live person. She liked to tell Sara and Rose what they *should* do. Rose knew it bothered Sara, but she also knew that Carol was just trying to help in her own way.

They had always been such a close family. Then Carol met Bill and they took off to California. Rose had always hoped that at some point what they called their "Adventure on the Left Coast" would be over and they would come to their senses and move back home to the saner Midwest. That never happened. Thirty years, three grandchildren, and one great grandchild later they were still in Southern California. Rose and Jack use to fly out to see them three or four times a year, and they would come back home once or twice a year, especially after the grandchildren were born. But in the five years between Jack's diagnosis and death, she saw them only twice.

After Jack died, Rose would go out and spend a week or two at Carol's, but she always got homesick. She didn't like that season-less climate. Plus, because she didn't see them very often, she felt awkward in their home. She wanted to help out, but felt she was getting in the way of their routine. She tried to spend time talking to her grandchildren, but once they got to be teenagers it was like pulling teeth. Not that Rose blamed them; they knew her only through birthday cards and gifts sent by mail and a couple of visits during the year. They wanted to hang out with their friends, not some old lady they barely know. How true. How sad.

Sara, on the other hand, had never strayed far from home.

Rose had always figured that if one of the girls was going to move away it would be Sara. She was the adventurous spirit, always trying something new, laying out her grand plans to graduate from college, travel the world, and do something extraordinary.

Then she met Steve. They fell in love, got married, bought a house, had children, and that was the end of that. No traveling the world, no extraordinary life—just marriage, kids, and a house. Seeing how her daughter with such big dreams had succumbed to a regular life, Rose wondered if Sara didn't sometimes feel stuck in her life. Of course she loved her life with Steve and the kids, but it sometimes seemed as though she wished she had been able to travel and see the world and have some adventures of her own. (And of course that didn't do anything to soothe the resentment she felt toward Carol, who had become a jetsetter.)

Not that raising a family isn't an adventure. Raising two kids while working full-time was quite an adventure. But Rose had always felt that Sara was missing something—even though she had achieved her career goals.

Now the poor girl had to deal with all of that and take care of Rose. "Dear Lord," she prayed, "is there any way we could do these last five years again...and maybe have things turn out so that I'm not such a burden?"

*A burden.*

Sara would never tell her all that. Not in so many words. But it was loud and clear nevertheless that Sara found it difficult to keep everything straight in her own life, much less have to take care of her mother, too.

Private time.... The feeling of loneliness washed over her once more like a great wave at high tide. Almost four years since Jack died...seemed like yesterday, seemed like forever ago. The doorbell sounded as Rose wiped the tears from her eyes. Lily was there.

# Chapter Five

# 9 a.m.

$S$ara rushed through the lobby of Olson Industries with barely a good morning nod in the direction of the receptionist. No time for courtesy this morning. She practically jogged down the hall to the elevator, and it was only after the door closed that she caught her reflection in the mirrored wall. *Oh my.* Her red face was contorted into a witchy scowl. She could feel the throb of her heartbeat in her head—a telltale signal that her blood pressure was redlining.

She drew in a deep breath and worked her face into a smile—put her game face on, got in game mode. *Game mode* was the image she projected to her co-workers and friends marked by a face with a bright smile, empathic ears eager to listen, and a mouth ready to share words of encouragement, praise, and thanks.

It was more or less real (or phony) depending on her mood. For the past year it had been phony more often than real. So this morning was no different from most. By the time the elevator came to a stop on the 12th floor, where her office suite was, she had her smile on. The doors opened, and she headed through the pool of cubicles greeting everyone she passed with a fairly convincing: "Happy Tuesday. How are you, Jim? Lauren? Maria? ... Just wonderful, thank you."

*Not exactly a performance that would score her an Oscar, but it was Work Sara, and it had worked so far.*

The reality was that she needed to be "on," and that meant the she could not—or at least *would* not—allow herself to bring any of her emotional baggage from home to the office. There was personal life and there was professional life...and she was determined that never the twain shall meet. Human Resources was all about keeping the workplace positive, and as the company's top HR officer, she had to model "positivity" from the top down.

That is what she was paid to do. She was *not* paid to model the very behaviors that contributed to low morale in the workplace. Maybe VP in her case stood for *Virtual Pollyanna.*

Sara had become an expert at controlling her feelings and casting an image. Her administrative assistant, Jane, even respectfully referred to her boss as *Saint Sara the Smiling.*

*Who took in her elderly mom to care for her?*

*Saint Sara.*

*Who took care of her children, her husband, and her home and then came to work to help even more people?*

*Why Saint Sara, of course.*

Good old Saint Sara, the friendly face of Olson Industries, Inc., as soft-hearted as she was hardworking.

She dropped her laptop case and purse on her desk and scanned over her daily planner open on her desktop. *Argh!* She had a meeting with the managers at 10 a.m. It was 9:50! The managers had requested a meeting to address their questions about the new benefits program roll-out before the all-hands meeting later in the day.

*You've been doing this for years*, she told herself. *Just relax.*

Instead of taking a wrong turn on memory lane on the way in to the office, she should have been doing some last-minute prep for the meeting—anticipating the questions they would ask and rehearsing her answers. She took a breath, grabbed her planner and the memo with the meeting agenda on it, and headed down to the 4th floor conference room.

It was her policy always to be the first one in the meeting room, whether she was moderating the meeting or not. On the way down in the service elevator (which would enable her another 45 seconds of peace to clear her head) she had the nagging suspicion—again—that something was missing. Missing with a big M. That feeling had been creeping up on her for some time now, maybe even since before her mother had come to live with them.

Even running late, she was the first one in the meeting room. She tried going through her pre-meeting calming ritual: taking in the sweeping view of the campus from the large picture window in the conference room. She let her eyes rest on the green lawn framed with maple and oak trees that lined the driveway and parking lot and which were now dripping with great gold and orange leaves that reflected on the calm surface of the retention pond. She scanned her eyes in search of one of the large white swans that glided across that pond so gracefully—hardly leaving any wake on the water. She always envied them their serenity. She knew that they had been put there to keep the Canada geese from nesting on the pond. If only she had an emotional swan to keep the geese of turmoil from nesting in her mind...and heart....

Before she was able to locate that little bevy of swans who lived out on the pond, Stan Westin, the company president, walked in, followed by a GM and a few of the managers with coffee in one hand and company-issue day-timers in the other. Stan joined her by the window and with a lowered voice, said, "Good morning, Sara. Could I have a moment of your time...before the meeting?"

"Of course you can, Stan," she said, flashing that big fake smile.

"It won't take but a minute…. In private."

"Oh, sure," she said.

He showed her out the side door of the conference room and led the way down the hall to a vacant office. He nodded toward a chair and she took it. He sat on the corner of the desk with his arms crossed. "It seems we have a bit of a problem."

"A problem?" she said, feeling her upper lip quiver a bit. That was always the trouble with fake smiles—they had a tendency to come undone at the most inopportune times.

"The meeting this afternoon at 1:00?"

"Yes."

"We have scheduling conflict. I just got back from Bangalore yesterday, and Louann told me that you had scheduled the all-hands meeting today from one to two o'clock. We have a manager's meeting scheduled from one to three this afternoon…."

Uh-oh. *Did I know that?*

"It's not a disaster," Stan told her. "Ordinarily, we would just push the manager's meeting back an hour, but we have the Q3 wrap-up call with our investors at 3:00, and of course that cannot be rescheduled."

"Of course it can't," she agreed. It wasn't a disaster, as he said, but it was a bit of a mess because many of the managers were traveling in from out of town, and the first manager's meeting of the quarter was always the longest. "I will take care of it," she assured him. "As soon as this meeting is over."

"Everybody makes mistakes," he told her. "Even you. I know how busy you have been and how hard you have worked on the benefits package."

"It's my job," she said, feeling disoriented. "I'm sorry, Stan. It's my bad."

"It's okay," he told her. "You'll come up with something. Come on."

At that moment Sara wasn't sure of anything...other than the suspicion that maybe she was out of her depths, that maybe she didn't really know what she was doing, that maybe she hadn't deserved that promotion after all. Stan Westin was a kind man, but he was also a perfectionist.

"Sara," he said, in a lowered voice, "you've been working too hard. Why don't you and Stuart take a vacation? You've been working too hard."

*Was he expressing genuine concern for her, or was he placing her on administrative leave? Don't you know, she thought, that this is my vacation? That Steve—not Stuart— and I couldn't take a vacation because we have mother to take care of?*

"I will take care of it, Stan," she said, rising to her feet and flashing that game face smile. "For every, *challenge* there is an opportunity to create a solution." If she was feeling out of sorts her smile would never give her away. She turned and headed back down that hall and into the conference room.

At the meeting—which, thank God, Stan Westin did not attend—she told the managers that they were going to put the present meeting in overdrive because the afternoon session would be for non-managerial personnel only. The managers had that *other* meeting to attend—the one hosted by their CEO Stan Westin. Sara spent the remainder of the hour giving the managers a condensed, one-hour version of the two-hour presentation she would give the non-managerial personnel later in the day.

She ended by telling them: "The two-hour meeting this afternoon will be videotaped and available to you on the company Intranet and, of course, I will be happy to address any concerns or answer any questions any of you might have. So read over the new benefits package, and call on me at any time."

After the meeting Sara grabbed her purse and headed up to the women's restroom in the executive suite where she knew she could be reasonably assured of some privacy. There she let it go and sobbed for a few minutes. But only for a few minutes. Then she pulled herself together, touched up her make-up, turned herself "on," and headed back to her office.

*This really wasn't that big of a deal—well, not a* great big *deal anyway. I can turn this into a win for our people. No problem.*

Problem one: solved.

Problem two: thinking.... She was supposed to give her brief "State of HR" address at Stan's quarterly manager's meeting. She couldn't be in two places at one time. She always made her speech during the second half of the manager's meeting. She would give the same condensed, one-hour presentation she had just given to the managers at the "all-hands" meeting at 1:00. Then she would go to the executive conference room and join Stan's manager's meeting at the halfway point—at 2:00. The second hour of the all-hands meeting would be for having fun and socializing. She would send her administrative assistant Jane out to buy 100 gallons of Blue Bell ice cream. They were going to turn the second half of the meeting into an ice cream social and Q&A session. Jane, who knew nearly as much about the new benefits package as Sara did, could field the questions and answer those she could and pass along those she couldn't.

Problem two: solved. She headed back to her office where she would meet with Jane, order lunch in, and tweak her PowerPoint presentation. Plan in place, she sat in her high-back executive chair, let out a big breath and let the soft leather nestle her, and started checking her voice- and e-mails.

*What is Missing...Missing...Missing...?*

# Chapter Six

# 9 a.m.

Even though Sara had given her a house key, Lily always insisted on ringing the doorbell and waiting for Rose to make her way in to the front door to let her in. It was hard to fault someone for being polite these days, Rose decided, and for all she knew it was a custom from the old country — Mexico, or was it Columbia? The Philippines, of course.

*Merciful heavens! You must be old if you're confusing Mexico with the Philippines.*

Though it was nice to see that some people still had manners, on mornings when her hip was afire, Rose could have done with a little rudeness if it meant she didn't have to get off the heating pad. She tried hollering, "Come on in, Lily, for heaven's sake." A moment passed, and the doorbell chimed again. Rose wondered if Lily even knew what she was saying. There were times when she asked for a ham sandwich and got grilled cheese.

*Why does she think Sara gave her that key?* Rose thought as she crossed the living room. The door bell chimed again. "I'm coming just as fast I can," she said. Then it dawned on her that this was probably one of Lily's creative ways of "helping" Rose get some exercise. If there's one thing I could do with less of, it's exercise, she thought, dreading her physical therapy session. *I could just fib and tell her I'm under the weather.*

Seconds later she was opening the front door, and there stood Lily in, what else, a pair of black slacks and bright-colored sweater (today it was orange). Lily always greeted Rose with the words, "Oh, Mama Rose, it is so good to see you," as if she were Rose's long-lost Filipino daughter.

"Hello, Lily," she said, proffering her cheek for a kiss. "Come on in before we both catch our death."

Lily was a petite woman of 25 years who had immigrated to the United States from the Philippines with her family six years back, so her accent was still thick and her English chipped if not broken. She was easy on the eyes and kept her long black hair pulled up in a bun the way women of Rose's generation had 50 years back. She dressed in a colored t-shirt or sweater and black pants.

She had a loving spirit and doted on Rose with genuine concern, but at times it could be a little bit much and would leave Rose feeling somewhat embarrassed. *Funny,* Rose thought, *how she praised other cultures for their respect of the elderly but found it a bit annoying up-close.* Rose had to tell Lily two or three times a day that she was perfectly capable of doing things for herself.

That wasn't true. It might not even have been true to say she was *somewhat* capable of doing *most* things for herself, but it was definitely true that she was capable of doing *some* things for herself.

Though Lily had been coming to the house five days a week for the past six months, Rose didn't want her helping out with bathing and dressing. So Rose made it a point to take her shower and get dressed before Lily got there.

A creature of habit, Lily stuck to her routine day by day. After making a little small-talk (no more, but rarely less, than 15 minutes) with Rose, she would get started on her housekeeping chores. Rose used to tell Sara that she didn't really need Lily to come "babysit" her every day. Then she realized that Lily's coming was at least as much for Sara's benefit as for Rose's. Sara liked having someone else clean her house, do her laundry, and buy her groceries. Rose, at Sara's age, couldn't stand for anyone to do any of that work for her. She didn't even like for Jack to do any work in the house that didn't require the use of power tools.

As Lily carried on with her chores, which always started in the kitchen, Rose sat in her rocker in the living room. This old rocker was the one thing that came from her home that was not stuffed in her bedroom. She liked to sit in it and watch TV or talk with the kids when they were home from college. It had belonged to her mother and her mother's mother before her. Three generations of women had rocked their babies to sleep in this chair. She had wanted to give it to Carol or Sara when they had their children, but they each politely said no because it didn't match their décor.

Funny how different things were when she had her girls. You didn't care as much about décor. Sure, you wanted things to be pretty and look neat and clean, but family heirlooms like chairs that had rocked generations of babies to sleep always seemed to fit into your decorating scheme.

Rose settled into the chair and looked around for the remote. There were several of them sitting on the table. Again she tried to figure out which one turned the channel. After several maddening moments pushing buttons on three different remotes she found the right one.She pretended to watch TV, all the while regretting that she was not able to do the housework so she could at least feel as though she were "earning her keep" in Sara's house.

Today, however, Rose was a little more content than usual just to sit. That dance move she made in the shower when she twisted to try to get that fresh bar of soap must have wrenched something. Her hip was burning. You might think that she looked forward to physical therapy on such a day—in the hopes that they would make a few adjustments to relieve the discomfort. You would be wrong. She had no use for that therapy. It only made things worse. Her hip was already hurting. By the time they had run her through the exercise routine everything else would be hurting, too. She had to figure out a way to get out of it—just for today.

She called Lily into the room.

"What is it, Mama Rose?"

"*It* is my hip. Please bring me one of my pain pills."

"Now Mama Rose, you know you not supposed to take that before exercise."

"No worry, I'm not going to 'exercise' today, so bring me that pill, please."

"Does Miss Sara know you not going? She didn't leave me any note."

"I am her mother, Lily, not the other way around. I can make my own decisions. It is my body they're going to be tearing limb-from-limb. So I'll thank you to just go in the kitchen and get me that pill, please."

"But Mama Rose, you know exercise is good for you, makes you stronger."

"What doesn't make me stronger kills me," she said. "Now, *please*, just get me that pill!"

Never one to raise her voice, she had learned that sometimes she had to be stern with Lily to let her know that, though Sara paid her salary, Rose was an adult woman who was able to make her own decisions. She had found through trial-and-error that this approach worked better than bribery. She had once offered Lily a $20 bill and told her she could leave an hour early if she would just cancel the bus that took Rose to therapy. She found out the hard way that Lily couldn't be bought.

Lily rolled her eyes. "Okay, Mama Rose, give me one minute."

Rose turned the TV volume down. Thanks to her hearing aid, she could hear Lily pick up the phone in the kitchen and begin dialing who else but Sara at work. That will never do.

"Lily, please come back in here for a moment."

"Comin', Mama Rose."

Rose heard her put the phone back in the cradle.

"Perhaps you are right. I need to go and exercise. I will take a pill or two when I get back home."

"Very good, Mama Rose."

Rose knew that Lily meant well, but on those occasions when she patronized Rose as if she were a little girl, Rose had to resist the urge to *accidentally* trip Lily with her cane—at least then that burdensome thing would be put to good use. Lily went back into the kitchen to her work, and Rose sat there in her chair brainstorming. She had to get one of those pills and she had to get out of going to therapy today. Her mind shifted to a conversation she recently had with Sara when she tried to explain how it felt to have lived for over 80 years, raised children, kept your home going, work part-time for an international company (hoping to relate closer to Sara's level), and now to have everyone treat you like a child. Sara said, "That's silly, Mother," and Rose said, "See, that right there. 'Silly' is what you say to a child who is acting foolish, not to a grown woman who taught you how to tie your shoes!"

She was the matriarch of the family—and to be treated like an addle-brained old fool or, worse, a little girl!

The girls used to come to her for advice. When they were in school, and even when they were young mothers, they would call Rose for her advice on boys, classes, careers, husbands, parenting, just about anything. Sara and Rose talked almost daily, especially after Jack died. Sara would stop over several times a week during her lunchtime or after work just to talk. To talk daughter-to-mother (where Sara was the daughter and Rose, the mother), woman-to-woman, friend-to-friend. Now Sara hardly had two words to share when she got home from work.

Funny how Sara could work in lunch with her mother at least twice a month before Rose moved in—when she lived in a neighboring town. Since Rose moved in there was no time for lunch in Sara's schedule. She came home late most nights and was so frazzled that she just plopped down on the sofa and watched TV. Rose missed the closeness they had always enjoyed, missed the conversations.

With Carol it was different; they had never been as close. Carol was, if anything, a daddy's girl. But Sara had always been right there, close by. Rose and Jack were at the hospital when Sally and Tommy were born. They spent birthdays and holidays with Sara and Steve and the kids. They were at the graduations and got together for dinner several times a month. They even went on several vacations together. What wonderful memories.

Now they were just that: memories. Rose now felt that there was nothing to look forward to, so all she could do was look back. No more trips to California; the whole ordeal of traveling was too much. No more family dinners; the kids were away at school, and Sara and Steve rarely talked when they did have a 15-minute sit-down dinner.

Rose decided to go to her room and lie down for a few minutes to take some pressure off of her hip. She had been up since 3 a.m. and she hoped she still had her secret stash of pain pills she kept hidden under the vanity in her bathroom just so if her hip acted up in the middle of the night she wouldn't have to go looking for them in the kitchen.

"O, Lily," she called out, "I'm a little tired. I think I'll just lie down for a little bit before 'exercise.'"

"Yes, Mama Rose, you take you some rest. I'll wake you for lunch so you eat something before you go exercise."

"I doubt I'll be too hungry," she said.

"Rest well, Mama Rose."

Rose pulled her bedroom door closed and went to the bathroom, felt under the vanity. There it was. She still had a few pills left. She needed to remember to get a few more from the bottle next time it was down so she wouldn't be out in the middle of the night when she needed it the most. Then she lay down on her bed, looked at the picture of Jack and her taken on their golden anniversary.

*So much is Missing....*

## Chapter Seven

# Noon

R ose was wakened by the sound of the phone ringing. She looked at the clock: 12:00. *Was that a.m. or p.m.?* Then she heard a knock on her door and Lily's voice calling, "Mama Rose, you' daughter is on the phone."

*Must be Sara making sure I am not trying to bribe my way out of therapy*, she thought. Lily handed her the phone.

"Hello."

"Hi, Mom."

It was Carol, not Sara. "Why hello there, stranger," she said, "how are you doing?"

"Oh, Mom, you know how it is here. Same old same old. Bill's latest kick is buying commercial properties. Says he's burned out on residential. I've been trying to talk him into retiring, but then what? He has so much energy. I am so ready to travel full-time! Patty and Kirk are so busy with their own lives that we're lucky if we see them once every few months. Little Kelly is going to be four next month. Can you believe that? Wish you could come out for her birthday."

"So do I," Rose said, feeling weary by the pace of the conversation much less the pace of Carol and Bill's life.

"Sorry, Mom, I know you're not up to traveling right now."

"No, not right now," Rose told her, thinking *it might be a while yet*. "What else is going on with you? Is Patty planning a big party for Kelly?"

"You know Patty," Carol said, "she's always going to extremes. She's having a princess party at a Tea Room in Montecito—that's where they live now. All of the little girls get to dress up like a princess and then play tea party...."

Rose tried to remember what her great-granddaughter Kelly looked like, but she just couldn't picture her. *Was she a towhead or a brunette? For that matter, what did Kelly's mother Patty, Rose's granddaughter, look like?*

"Well, they'll have a big time, I'm sure," Rose said.

They went on talking for another five or 10 minutes, just making the kind of chit-chatty conversation that Rose would love to be able to share with Sara, before Carol finally asked The Question: "So how are you, Mom—*really*?"

Carol called twice a month and always asked The Question a few minutes into the conversation. Not that she could do anything about it—whether Rose said she was doing well or ill. She was half way across the country.

"Oh, I'm okay," Rose lied. Then she said, "I'm just feeling a little tired."

"Tired. Oh? Are you taking the vitamin-packs I sent you?"

"I might be," Rose said, and added quickly, "I've got a pain in the rump—my hip—that is acting up, so I've been trying to get plenty of rest today. I was actually taking a nap when you called."

"Mother, why didn't you say something? Do you want me to let you go?"

"No, honey. It was about time for me to get up and have lunch anyway. I sure am dreading going to physical therapy. My leg is already throbbing, and all that rigmarole just makes it worse."

"Then why on earth are you still going? If it isn't making you feel better or helping you get stronger then maybe you should think about finding another way to exercise."

"I've thought about taking up tennis."

"Mother!" Carol laughed.

"Or maybe aerobics. Sara has a Richard Simmons video called *Sweatin' With The Oldies.* That might be just my speed."

"I think it's *Sweatin'* To *The Oldies*," Carol corrected, still chuckling.

"Something like that," Rose said.

"Seriously, though, Mother, if the therapy is causing pain then they are doing it wrong."

"Well, Sara says it will help me to keep going. She had the doctor tell me that last time I was there after I told them I didn't want to go anymore. I asked him if by law they could force me to go."

"Well, I know Sara means well, Mother," Carol said, "but if you are in pain, why would the doctor tell you to keep going?"

"Beats me, honey. But that's what he said. So I have to go."

Carol was ever her advocate—from 1,500 miles away. "You really don't have to do anything you don't want to, Mom. I mean you're not a kid."

"I know, honey, but I don't want to upset Sara."

"Well Sara isn't the one in pain, Mother: *You* are! Do you want me to speak to her about this?"

*Uh-oh, now I've done it.* "No, no, honey, it's fine. I will speak with Sara about it tonight. Please don't make waves...."

"Are you afraid of Sara, Mother?"

"Of course I'm not, Carol," Rose told her. "You asked how I was and I told you, but don't worry."

"Well, I will...."

95

"Everything will be fine."

"I have to run. Bill just pulled up and we have an appointment with a developer at 9:30."

After she hung up with Carol, Rose thought: *I will talk to Sara tonight...and I hope to heavens Carol doesn't call her. She tried that before and, like the physical therapy itself, her best efforts only made things worse.*

Rose took the phone into the kitchen and just before putting it in its cradle she spotted the number for the senior shuttle and physical therapy clinic on the side of the refrigerator. Lily was in the basement laundry room washing clothes. Rose first dialed the number to the senior shuttle and told the person who answered that she wasn't feeling good and needed to cancel. The person thanked her for calling and hoped she felt better and confirmed her Thursday pick up. That was the easy call. The shuttle bus is only for seniors so they are used to the "old folks" canceling because they don't feel good. Now to call the physical therapy clinic — Rose double-checked the number on the LCD screen before hitting send. It had become more difficult for her to dial the phone over the years. The buttons had gotten smaller and her hands, more gnarled with age.

She got the voicemail at the therapy center. They must have been at lunch: *Perfect.* At the beep, she left her message: "Yes, uh, hello, this is Mrs. Rose Barnes.... I'm not feeling good, so I won't be at therapy today. Thank you. Have a nice day."

A moment later Lily come back into the kitchen. "Did you have a nice talk with you' daughter?"

"Charming. Now Lily, I am going to sit out on the front porch and enjoy the brisk autumn air before the bus comes to take me to therapy." Without waiting for a reply, Rose turned and headed for the door.

*How on earth had it come to this? Lying like a little child to get out of going to therapy. When did she stop being able to make her own decisions or, more importantly, when did people stop taking her decisions seriously?*

She knew that Sara really was trying to do what was best for her, but it only added to her feelings of inadequacy.

"But.... Mama Rose—"

Rose pretended she didn't hear her and continued towards the door.

As she made her way through the door, Rose thought: Free at last! She tried to recall the last time she had exercised any authority at all. Recently she spent most of her time following the direction of others. She went out on the front porch and sat down in a cushioned wicker chair and let the crisp breeze wash over her. The leaves on the trees were changing and the days were getting shorter. Autumn was Rose's favorite season. She loved everything about it—the smell of the brown leaves on the grass and the sight of the flowers with amazing colored blooms. She looked around at the landscaping in front of the house. The mums were coming in at the foot of the porch in beautiful shades of yellow, orange, rust, and maroon.

A horn honked and she looked up to see the postal carrier bringing her mail jeep to a stop. She hopped out with a bundle of mail and head up the walkway toward the porch. Rose still received the occasional piece of mail at her new "permanent address." Every single one was addressed to Mrs. Jack Barnes.

The greatest day of Rose's life was the day she became Mrs. Jack Barnes, yet since his death it had been difficult for her to see that name written on anything. After his death it was if she had lost her identity. Nothing seemed the same, not even her name. She was a widow, the wife of a dead man. It seemed so odd that all these years later it still didn't seem real.

For some reason the mail always reminded her of Jack's funeral, and today was no exception. The funeral was difficult. It was bad enough that she had to bury the love of her life—her husband of 55 years—but to see him put on display, not him but his lifeless corpse, so thin, so wasted, his skin so papery thin, for all of their friends and family to see. She and the girls disagreed about the funeral. They wanted a two-day wake and funeral with an open casket. She wanted a one-day wake and funeral with a closed casket. They wanted to make sure everyone who loved them could come and say goodbye to him. Rose just wanted to breathe again.

In the end they compromised—once Carol was able to make it home. A one-day wake with an open casket. It was odd, but until the day of his funeral she hadn't noticed how the disease had eaten away at his body. It didn't even look like him lying there in the casket, so cold, so small. She didn't want the people who loved him to remember him like that. She wanted them to remember him as he was before Alzheimer's. She wanted them to remember the funny, lively, healthy Jack whose smile could heal every wound.

To her it was as if she had taken a deep breath the day the doctor told them Jack's diagnosis and had held it until he breathed his last. She had thought that if she could get through the funeral then maybe she would be able to breathe again. Now that it was over, she just wanted to be done with the fuss as quickly as possible—it was like ripping a bandage off in one quick pull so it doesn't hurt as much.

After it was over, she realized that it wouldn't have mattered if the wake and funeral were one-day or one-month long, the pain of the experience was still crushing.

She couldn't even recall most of the mourners who came to pay their final respects to Jack that day. They were just a sea of more or less sorrowful, more or less familiar, faces each taking hold of her hands and parroting some variation on the theme: "So very sorry for your loss." Over and over: "So very sorry for your loss."

Rose didn't cry that day. She was too numb to cry. She just nodded and said, "Thank you," and then looked at the clock on the wall to see how much more of this she had to bear.

The day she started breathing again was also etched into her memory. It was April 29. The sun was bright that day and she decided to spend some time out in the yard. As she approached the garden she noticed a fresh bloom of what Jack used to call Laughing Daisies had blossomed almost overnight. They were so vibrant with color and full of life. She felt as if it were Jack saying to her, "Look, my Rose, I sent you some Laughing Daisies to brighten your day. I'm where I am whole again. Breathe."

After she moved in, Steve, the sweetheart, had built her a raised garden bed so that she could still plant flowers without having to bend over. She tried to plant seasonally, but it was hard on her. She had to rely on Sara or Steve to take her to the nursery. They were both so busy and she hated to bother them. She was at the age, she thought, when it might be a good idea to stick with perennials....

## Chapter Eight

# Noon

S ara was at her desk picking at the Chef's salad she had delivered from the deli a block away. She was eating it because she needed to—to get her strength up for the meeting—certainly not because she wanted to. She had no appetite at all.

Her cell phone rang. She looked at the number: 805 area code. Santa Barbara. It was Carol. *Great…just great. Carol had always had an impeccable sense of timing—bad timing.*

She hit the talk button: "Carol?"

"Sara? Carol. What's going on with Mom?"

So much for the icebreaker…maybe *How are you doing? Or How's the weather there in God's country?* Carol's question seemed leading to Sara, which is exactly what she did not need right now. Suddenly she flashed angry.

"What do you mean—*what's going on with Mom?*"

"I just got off the phone with her and she seems depressed and lonely. She said all she does is sit around all day by herself. I thought you had someone coming in to sit with her?"

Not the weekly unsolicited advice call. Funny how easy it was for Sister Carol the Saint to dispense long-distance advice yet never lift a finger to do anything. *Did she ever once ask about Sara's life? No. Never. Never asked about her work, her husband, her kids.*

"Gee, Sis, thanks for your concern. Lily is there this morning with Mother, just as she is every weekday, and Mother is going to therapy this afternoon just as she does every Tuesday and every Thursday. I gave you her itinerary before."

"That therapy is another thing," Carol said. "Mom said that you and the quack you've got her going to told her that, by law, she is required to go and endure very painful therapy without her consent."

"*What?!* Nobody ever told her any such thing. That is ridiculous, Carol. Even you are not that gullible."

"No need to get snippy with me, Sara. I'm just trying to help."

*Help? Trying to help? That's a good one!*

*How could you help us?* Let me count the ways. Help would be…sending a little money every month to help cover the cost of Lily's services. Help would be…flying out to see Mother every few months or over the holidays. Help would be…not calling to criticize someone who *is* trying to help.

Sara knew that if she didn't cut the conversation short she was going to tell her "helpful" big sister just exactly what she really thought. "Carol, I am in the middle of preparing for a very important meeting here at Olson—"

"What could be more important than caring for your own mother?"

"Thanks for the call Carol, I have to go. Talk to you soon"

With that, she hung up the phone.

Time was wasting, and she still had a lot to do to prep for the meeting, but she picked up the phone and called home to find out what in fact was *going on with Mom….*

# Chapter Nine

# 12:30 p.m.

R ose, still sitting out on the porch enjoying the Autumn day, heard the phone ring in the house, and a moment later Lily opened the front door and said, "Mama Rose, Miss Sara is on the phone, and she don't sound happy."

"I hope everything is okay," Rose said, suspecting that she had been found out.

*Uh-oh,* Rose thought, maybe the therapy center had called *her* to verify *my* cancellation.

She took the phone from Lily and said, "Hi honey, is everything okay."

"Mother, what is going on?"

"Nothing much," Rose told her.

"I just got off the phone with Carol ..."

*Uh-oh.*

"...who wanted to know why I was forcing our mother to go to therapy when she is in pain. She said that you told her that Dr. Peterson and I—and Mother, he is *not* a quack—told you that it was federal law that you had to go to therapy. Then the therapy clinic called and said that you canceled."

*Word travels fast.*

"So, Mother, what is going on?"

"I don't know why Carol took a notion to call you. I asked her not to. I just told her that I woke up with a little pain in my leg today and was tired and didn't want to go to therapy. That's all. And, well, yes, I did call the clinic and told them to cancel my appointment."

"Mother, you can't just cancel your therapy every time you decide you don't feel like going."

"That would be *every* time," Rose told her.

"They have a schedule and you are supposed to call at least 24 hours in advance to cancel. They have a waiting list, and the therapist said they would have to stop treating you if you keep canceling."

"What could be worse?" Rose said.

"Mother, I did a lot of research, made a lot of calls, and took a lot of tours to find the right clinic that could help you get stronger...."

"And I thank you for it, Sara, but I can't help it when I don't feel good. I'm sure they understand it when old people don't feel good and can't get out. Besides, I am an adult and can still make decisions for myself."

"Fine, Mother," Sara said. "Whatever you want.... Love you, Mother. Talk to you later."

Rose felt guilty, she almost called the clinic and told them that she was feeling better and would keep her appointment after all, but as she turned to pick up the phone again she felt that tinge of pain in her hip and decided to leave well enough alone. She made a deal with herself that she could stay home today but had to go Thursday, no matter how she felt.

Rose went back to the front porch and sunk back into the chair. *I'm an adult. I just want to take one day off from therapy.* She settled into the seat and closed her eyes and began to pray. "Dear God, why does it have to be so hard? Just give me some peace. Help me to understand my daughter. Help my pain to go away, Lord, so that I can help out more and not be such a burden. Thank you for loving me. Amen."

Rose always felt a peace that passes understanding after praying. She wondered why she didn't pray more. It always seemed to help her calm down.

Sunday had always been the best day of the week for the Barnes family. She and Jack would get up on Sunday morning and make a big breakfast—bacon, eggs, toast, pancakes, fresh-squeezed orange juice—for the girls. Then off to church they would go to the little congregational church in which the girls were baptized, confirmed, and married. Both of Sara's children—Sally and Tommy—were baptized and confirmed there as well.

Jack's funeral was held in that church—and one day soon hers would be too.

Sunday afternoon at the Barnes' house was always family time. Extended family would come from all over, as well as friends and neighbors, all bringing a covered dish. Everyone would eat, clean up the table and dishes, and then put everything back out several hours later and eat again, and there were always leftovers for everyone to take home. It was Family Feast Day and the special occasion was: It was Sunday, of course.

Rose had never questioned the existence of God. From early in life she had always sensed Him there. So God was a given in her life. Even when Jack was diagnosed with Alzheimer's she prayed and thanked God for the time that they had together. After he was gone, Rose found comfort in prayer, a real sense of peace in resting in her faith that if God was in control she didn't have to be.

Carol and Sara had a harder time with it and seemed angry with God over Jack's Alzheimer's. They continued to go to church every week—Sara to the church she had grown up in, which made it nice for Rose, who still got see her friends at church every Sunday, and Carol to a very large, "progressive" church in southern California. The music was a little loud and not as catchy as the old standard hymns Rose enjoyed, but they loved Jesus all the same.

One thing that troubled Rose was the fact that after Jack's death both of her daughters had gone from being actively involved in different areas of ministry to just being attendees. It made Rose sad. She prayed for them to turn back to Him for comfort.

A few minutes later Lily came out the front door and stood in front of Rose.

"Just wanted to see if you needed anything before you' bus comes."

"Not coming today, Lily. I gave them the day off," Rose told her, knowing full well that Lily made sure she was doing her "cleaning" in close proximity when Rose was on the phone and already knew that she wasn't going to therapy today.

"Does Miss Sara know?"

"Now, Lily, you know full well that Sara knows! Mommy said I don't have to go." Rose realized that her sarcasm was sharp and should not have been directed at Lily, who was only trying to help.

"I'm sorry, Lily; I didn't mean to be that short with you. Sara knows I'm not going. I am just in too much pain today."

"Then it's a good thing you took the pain pill you keep under you' sink when you went into you' room," Lily said with a smile.

"How did you know I took a pain pill? I mean I didn't...."

Lily laughed. "Oh Mama, you not too good at the lies. I know that look on you' face when you gonna do something you' not suppose to. Like call and cancel the exercise." Lily's smile grew bigger.

"You are good, Lily," Rose told her with a smile. "I have to give you credit for that. You are good."

"You daughter just want the best for you. Miss Sara just want you to be healthy and strong. She loves you so much. That's why she wanted you to live here with her and her family. So she can take care of you."

"I know, Lily. Sara loves me. It's just sometimes.... Oh, never mind."

"It's just sometimes you feel like you a child. Like she's the Mama and you are her daughter. You don't think people listen to you. They do listen to you. They just busy people. They tryin' to do the best they can. I know it's hard for you to have other people take care of you. From the stories you and Miss Sara and Mister Steve tell me you have always been the rock of your family. You always been the one takin' care of everyone else, but now it's time for you to let them take care of you back."

"You are pretty insightful for being such a young thing," Rose told her.

"You sure can be a troublemaker for being such an old thing."

They both laughed. Lily often surprised Rose by somehow knowing exactly what she was up to and what she was trying to get away with.

Lily seemed to have a heart for working with older people. She remembered the first day that Lily came to the house for the interview. Sara had interviewed a number of people, all of whom Rose quickly dismissed. Sara would interview them in the living room while Rose listened in from the kitchen. She would make her lists of what she didn't like about them and then Sara would bring in the next contestant. Rose almost felt as if it were a reality show called *Who will Care for the Old Lady....*

Then Lily showed up at the door.

Sara opened the door and introduced herself. After shaking Sara's hand, Lily instinctively walked passed her into the kitchen to where Rose was sitting and sat down next to her. Rose remembered the confused look on Sara's face as she entered the kitchen behind her trying to figure out a polite way to bring her back into the living room for her formal interview. Lily, however, had enough insight to know that though Sara asked the questions Rose was the one who she would be taking care of.

She politely told Sara, "I know you have questions you want to ask, but I thought you should ask them in here with your Mama so she doesn't have to strain so hard to listen to the answers."

Both Sara and Rose were caught off-guard. Rose remembered Sara's face as she looked at her. The look on her face was the final straw that had sent Rose into a laughing spell. Unassuming little Lily had caught onto Sara's game and noticed the man behind the curtain. Her hysterics had then sent Sara into a belly laugh as Lily sat there smiling.

She was hired right away. She has been a gift to Rose ever since.

Lily packed up her bag and headed out the door. "Bye Mama, see you tomorrow. Enjoy your day off."

"Bye, Lily," Rose called back as she watched Lily get into her car.

As Lily pulled away she honked her horn, smiled, and waved. Rose thought about what it must be like for someone coming from another country to America. From her conversations with Lily she surmised that they had not had much more than a dream of a new life when they arrived here.

Poor thing then had to spend five days a week looking after an old lady and someone else's house, yet she managed to do it all with a song in her voice and a smile on her lips. Lily never seemed to be in a bad mood. And though Rose didn't always appreciate her, she had to admit that Lily had become part of the family.

Rose sat for another moment thinking about Lily and the dream of a new life. Those kind of big dreams were all things of the past for Rose. All she had today were her memories.

# Chapter Ten

# 2 p.m.

Sara made it through the meeting with her game face on and actually turned it into a win not only for the HR department, her own baby, but for Olson Industries. Back in her office with the door closed and locked behind her, and having given Jane strict orders to hold all calls, she laid her head down on the desktop and whispered, "God, please help me. Everything is falling apart."

She had never felt like such a slacker. Not long ago she had looked forward to these meetings. She would put extra thought into them, making sure there were plenty of fun items on the agenda to achieve just the right mix of pleasure with business. She would have original trivia games with prizes and gift certificates and achievement certificates. A favorite was the *Whose Baby Picture Is It?* contests at the expense of the company's management team.

Lately, however, she had been slapping the agenda together at the last minute when there was no time for adding any fluff. People used to look forward to her meetings, now they all looked like they had been summoned to the gallows. There was never a spare minute for creativity. It was all she could do most days to keep from coming apart at the emotional seams. Maybe this is how menopause starts....

All Sara wanted to do after a long day topped off with fighting evening rush-hour traffic was have something to eat and sit on the couch like a mindless blob and watch TV.

Mother was bored during the day, despite the fact that she had Lily there to keep her company. Sara would love to be able to spend her day sitting around chumming it up with someone like Lily, who was very different from the people she got to interact with all day. Not that the Olson staff was bad; there were some truly wonderful people on the company roll. But the HR department, by design, was the internal customer support desk, a/k/a the official "complaint department." She was the one they came to when they had an issue. Her staff was competent, but she had done them a disservice in some ways by always promoting what she called a "very wide open door policy," so it was sometimes easier for them to come to her than to develop effective HR problem-solving skills.

It had backfired.

Used to be, she enjoyed the challenges and wouldn't have it any other way. When she could settle a dispute or help someone find resources they needed to make them better at their job Sara would come alive. Now the game face had become nothing more than a mask, and she was finding it harder and harder to deal with the day-to-day issues.

At first she had thought it was the promotion—"comes with the territory: more responsibility, more pressure, more visibility, more accountability"—but that was what she had been working for all along. *Wasn't it?* She knew what the job entailed and could do most of it with her eyes closed, but this morning: what a wake-up call. Standing there before Stan Westin, having dropped the ball, she had felt just like a little girl.

She could feel the weight of the stress on her from every facet of her life. Trying to keep up with the demands of her career, the distance she felt growing between her and Steve, the change in her role with her mother from daughter to caregiver.

*It is amazing how much things can change in such a short amount of time. How did it all get to be so overwhelming? Where did I miss the sign that said "Danger Ahead"?!*

She loved her mother so much, and she and Steve knew it was the right thing to do having her move in. She wouldn't have had it any other way. But it was also true to say that she couldn't have realized how much help and attention her mother would need. Even knowing what she knew now, however, she couldn't even think about her mother having to live in a nursing home. One of her co-workers had told her that there were a lot of resources and other types of living arrangements for seniors. They gave her phone numbers of assisted living communities and other local agencies, but after all of the time and energy Sara put into just finding the right therapy center, she couldn't bring herself to make the calls. Just the thought of doing all of the research weighed her down emotionally.

It had broken her heart watching her mother sit at her father's bedside day after day, week after week, month after month, holding his hand, saying nothing. She couldn't help but contrast that with the way she had known them all her life—always poking at each other, holding hands, whispering and giggling like two love-struck teens. It was so strange when she would go to her friends' homes when she was growing up and their parents didn't really have anything to say to each other or, sometimes, snapped at each other instead of talking. On the other hand, some of her friends thought it was strange that Sara's parents were so close and genuinely enjoyed each other.

Even before she was old enough to play dress-up, she knew that she wanted a marriage just like her parents had. And she had it in Steve—*had* being the operative term. Steve had always known how to make her smile; they never walked anywhere together without holding hands. They used to take nightly walks around the block and smile when their elderly neighbor Mr. Warner would whistle and teasingly call out, "Wonder when those two lovebirds are going to tie the knot—what? They're already married, and they still hold hands." They hadn't had time for their walks since Rose moved in. She was aware of a growing rift between them. Some nights, they didn't seem to have much of anything to say to each other much less to talk about during a 20-minute walk.

Who had 20 minutes these days? It seemed like there was always something to help mother with, and Sara was just too exhausted emotionally and physically to make it around the block. She *missed* that time with Steve. It seemed that lately they were always running past each other, on their way in and out of the door.

With both of the kids in college, this was supposed to be their "empty nest" time when at last they would have the house all to themselves and would be free to act like "crazy kids," as Steve called it. He had threatened for years to spend most of his time prancing around the house in his drawers!

So much for all that.

Mother always told Sara and Steve to go out to dinner and take in a movie or at least take a walk. It was important, she said, for them to have time alone with each other without "some old woman lurking about," but Sara always worried. What if they left her alone and something happened? What if she fell and lay there for hours waiting for them to come home from a date? How would she be able to forgive herself if that happened—*again?*

Yes, there was some residual guilt about the day her mother fell and broke her hip. Mother had called on the Friday before the Monday she fell and told Sara that she had turned her ankle and was icing it down and favoring it so that it would get better. Sara had been so preoccupied with the upcoming executive conference that she didn't do what a good and faithful daughter *should* have done — go over and insist that she go for X-rays, maybe get it splinted, and bring her home for bed rest (or at least plenty of assistance) until it was completely well.

She had done no such thing. She just said, "Well, go easy on it," and left it at that. She could picture so vividly how it must have happened; Mom, favoring her hurt foot, slipping on the bathroom rug and breaking her hip.

Nothing she could do to change it now…except use it as Exhibit A to prove the case that she was not a good daughter. If only she had been more attentive then maybe, just maybe, mother would still be living at 117 Mitchell Place and enjoying her active social life. Maybe they would still be able to enjoy each other's company without all the anger and resentment.

There was a gentle knocking at her office door. She stood up, smoothed her suit, and stretched her eyes. Quick check of her make-up. It was a mess. "Sara?" It was the voice of Heidy, the only real friend she had at Olson. Heidy was a Marketing Director and had an uncanny insight about situations and an uncanny way of becoming instant friends with most everyone she came in contact with. She also had a gift for asking the right questions that allowed her to somehow move past external small talk and get inside you to what she referred to as "the good stuff." Spending time with her was almost like being in the confessional.

Sara remembered Heidy's interview and how they had hit it off immediately. They started off as just work friends, making time every day to share office gossip and catch up from the weekend. Sara enjoyed hanging out. They had a lot in common — starting with the overachiever personalities. Heidy was about the same age, and she and her husband Dennis had two kids who had just headed off to college. They could relate to each other. It only took six months for them to start hanging out as couples, coming over for barbeques, celebrating each other's birthdays. Heidy always knew when Sara was on overload and always knew how to cheer her up. She would often leave funny cards on Sara's desk or cut out comics and tape them to her computer.

Sara got up from her desk, trying to pull herself together before opening the door. Not that she thought she could fool Heidy into thinking everything was okay.

She opened the door and showed Heidy in, then closed the door and locked it. "Have a seat."

"Is everything okay?" Heidy asked.

"Fine," Sara lied. "Why do you ask?"

"Really?"

"I'm fine," Sara said, a little too forcefully.

Heidy sat down on the leather chair across the desk from Sara. "You know what *fine* stands for, don't you? Frustrated, Irritated, Neurotic, and Exhausted."

"Nice to know I wasn't lying after all," Sara told her, and for the first time that day, she smiled.

"You just didn't seem yourself in the meeting today."

"Who did I seem like?"

"Ever seen *The Stepford Wives*?"

"Good one," Sara said.

"It was kind of like you were just going through the motions."

*The emotions was more like it.*

Heidy continued. "That's not like you at all, Sara. I mean, you're the only person I have ever known who gets excited about an all-hands meeting."

"I don't get out much," Sara told her. "Ah, who am I kidding? Heidy, we're off the record, right?"

"Always."

"The truth is, I just can't seem to get myself together lately. I keep dropping the ball, and most times I don't even

116

*see* the ball coming before it hits me in the face. It's so hard. There's a lot going on...that I haven't—"

"Shared with anybody here at work?"

"Right." Sara leaned back in her chair and let her head fall back into the soft leather. "You're so smart."

"That's true," Heidy said, amused with herself, "but it doesn't take any Einstein to see that you're stressing."

Sara sighed. "I just don't know how to get it all done now."

"How are things going with your mom?"

"Fine...according to your definition of the word," Sara told her. "Oh, Heidy, I'm so overwhelmed. Between, home, work, and now Mom, it's just too much. I never seem to get caught up, and nothing I ever do is enough, let alone *good* enough. Sometimes when I leave here in the evening—or when I leave home in the morning—I feel like hitting the interstate and just driving as far away from here as I can get, take on an assumed identity, get away from it all."

"Guess the Calgon's not working," Heidy said.

Sara smiled. "I wish. It's just that I can't seem to do anything for anyone without somehow messing it up. I've become this stark-raving mad woman who's intolerant of the very people I love the most. Half the time here at work I'm tasting blood from having to bite my tongue to keep from going off on someone. I don't know, it's like I hear people's issues all day long and then I go home and have to deal with mother's issues or my stupid sister calls to bless me out about how *I* am not doing enough."

Heidy was nodding, so easy to talk to, so safe. "You're under a lot, Sara."

"It's not that I don't care."

"Of course it isn't."

"It's just that I feel like I can never get a break from having to solve everyone's issues and it's pushing me to the brink of—what?—a nervous breakdown. On the way in this morning an SUV cut me off and I had a little road rage episode. I cussed like a sailor! I've become a complete b-i-t-c-h. See? Right there. Wasn't that the first profanity you've ever heard me utter?"

"Yes it was, though I don't know if spelling the word counts," Heidy said. "Listen, Sara, you are the best person I know. It's true that you are always there for everyone—but you don't have to be. We will all love you just as much—maybe more—if you're on the receiving end of a little help and support sometimes."

"That's a good one," Sara said.

"No, really, you're the best, Sara—the *real* Sara."

"How would anybody know the real Sara? It's all fake! I'm a phony."

"You'll never convince me of that—unless maybe if I cut you off in my SUV sometime."

"You drive a Lexus, Heidy."

"I can still cut you off in it," Heidy said. "Seriously, Sara, everybody has a game face. Even I do. You don't think I'm the same person at home as I am here at Olson, do you? You of all people know I'm not!."

"But I used to love being around people—coaching them through their challenges. Now I just want to tell them to get the he— ck out of my face and give them a quarter to call someone who cares."

"First, a call costs more than a quarter and most people have cell phones these days. Besides, who hasn't wanted to say that?" Heidy asked, staring at Sara as if she knew she was about to get Sara to spill the "good stuff." "It's not like you're Mother Teresa. Stop being so hard on yourself, will you? You have a lot on your plate. Most of us go home and relax in the evening. When you go home your second shift starts."

It felt so good to vent, to have somebody to talk to who really cared. Sara felt the way she used to feel when she and her mother were close. Rose Barnes was the living proof that what Heidy had said was true because her mother loved her when she was being herself, when the mask was off (the "goody-goody-let's-pretend-we're-perfect" mask and the "angry-bitter-short-fused-mean-spirited" mask).

Sara said, "The worst part of the whole thing is that my mom and I used to be so close. We would talk almost every single day, but since she moved in we hardly talk at all. We have grown farther and farther apart. It's so hard; it's killing me. Our entire relationship has changed. It's like she is mad at me for everything I try to do, and I just can't seem to do anything right. So I think, well, I'll go where I know that I am competent and I get here and I screw up like I did double-booking the managers' meetings. It feels like I just can't do anything right anymore."

Heidy scooted her chair closer to the desk and lowered her voice. "You know, Sara, to be honest I can't even imagine what it's like for you to have to deal with all of the things you take on each day. But I want to say a couple of things. First, stop beating yourself up about the meeting today. I'm probably the only one in the whole company who even noticed that you didn't seem quite like yourself and that's because I know you so well. Second, I know it's been difficult since your mother moved in. I know you struggle to meet her needs; I can see it every time you talk about her. But, to be fair, I don't think it's like your mother woke up one day and said, 'Gee, I think I'll slip and fall today and break my hip so I'll have to be completely dependent on Sara and go live with her and disrupt her entire life and lose all of my dignity and become a royal burden. Yes, that's what I'll do.' I mean, Sara, as frustrated as you are, I am sure that she must be just as frustrated. Imagine what it's like to walk in her shoes— having to have somebody do things that you have done for yourself your whole life."

"Well...," Sara said.

"Think about it," Heidy said.

"I guess it's strange that I've never really thought about it like that before. I run through my day oblivious that there are other people involved. I only see them from the perspective of what they need and want from me—not from how they must feel. It's hard for me to look at it from her perspective. I mean, from my perspective, it looks pretty nice about now—to have everyone do everything for me, to cater to my every need...."

"To lose the love of your life?" Heidy added. "To lose your ability to get around? Not be able to live in your own home? To know every moment of every day that your best years are behind you? To know that you were never going to get any of the things you lost back? To know that you have become a burden, not a delight, to your daughter?"

Sara dropped her face in her hands and wept in great heaving sobs. Of course her mother was miserable. Rose Barnes always prided herself on her independence. She wasn't one to sit back and let others cater to her. She was the one doing the catering. "Mom was always the one who was seeing what she could do for others. When my oldest, Sally, was born Mom was there every day to help me learn how to bathe, feed, and diaper the babies, to show me hold to hold them and rock them and love them. She was always so sweet and patient with me. She never made fun of newbie mom me. She was just like an angel sent from heaven to me, there every day helping to care for the kids, yet still allowing me to be in charge of the process."

Heidy smiled, though her own eyes were damp. She said, "And so when she needed help, you took her in. That's what we do, Sara. We love and care and support one another."

"Sara," Heidy said, "I know you love your mother. You don't have to convince me. I'm just concerned that you are taking on too much. And forgive my bluntness, but most of it is your own fault. You think you always have to be some type of Human Resource SuperHero who can single-handedly solve all the company's—if not all the world's—problems while your staff sits around looking for something to do...and when you do give them something to do you are frequently micromanaging the process. I'm not piling on here. Listen, Sara, you do it because you are committed to what you do and that's great. But it puts all of the responsibility on you and doesn't empower your staff to take on new projects and take stuff off of your plate. You need to set boundaries and DELEGATE!"

"You really think so?"

"I know so! The ironic thing is that I actually learned that at one of your in-services. I actually listen."

"I really hate it when my good teaching gets thrown back in my face," Sara said.

"I'm just saying...," Heidy said. "Let's see. How can I break this to you? Here goes. I hate to be the one to have to break this news to you, Sara, but you are human. There is no magic wand and you do not have superhero powers."

"Really?"

"I thought it would be better if you heard if from someone else who had to find out the hard way that she can't fly. Sad day for all of us when we find that out."

"Depends on how far up you are when you try to." Sara and Heidy both let out a laugh, then Heidy got up and gave Sara a hug.

"You are going to be okay. I promise."

After Heidy left, Sara sat there alone for a long while wondering why she had never tried to see the events of the past five years from her mother's perspective. *Why had it been all about her?*

Before leaving the office for the evening, she sent an e-mail to her whole HR staff. She called a meeting for later in the week so they could jointly develop a plan for the staff to take on some of Sara's projects that would help them achieve success and build their resumes. That, after all, was the very reason she had taken the position in the first place, to help others achieve their goals. Her supervisors had done that for her throughout her career, so now it was her turn to do that for those who worked for her.

It would be hard, of course. She was the poster girl for Type A personality. But Heidy was right. She needed to delegate more, and she needed to start taking care of herself. She finished up her immediate tasks and decided the rest of the piles on her desk could wait until tomorrow. She shut off her computer and office light and headed for the car.

As she merged onto the freeway her cell phone rang. It was Steve. "Hi, sweetheart," he said, in a very cheerful voice.

"Steve?" she said. "Where are you?" This was always the question she asked him first. She always hoped he would say "at home" so she would not have to walk into the house and deal with her mom alone.

"I'm fine," he said, teasing. "Oh, you asked *where* I am not *how* I am."

"Now Steve. That was going to be my next question."

"Well, I answered that one already, so I'm on my way home from my meeting. It ran a little late, but everything went awesome and I got the contract."

"That's great news, Steve," she said, trying to remember what contract he was up for. "That's exciting."

"Well, don't wreck the car in all that excitement," he said. She wasn't the only one in the family with the *gift* of sarcasm.

"I am excited, Steve," she said. "It's just been quite a day."

"In that case," he said, "how about if I pick up some lasagna and ziti at Provino's so you don't have to worry about cooking dinner tonight?"

"But wait, you're the one we're celebrating," she told him.

He made a psssh-ing sound as if his cell phone connection were breaking up. "What's that you want some Risotto di Giorno, too? Sure."

"Steve?"

"Pssshhhhh. We're breaking up."

"I'd never break up with a wonderful man like you."

"I love you, Sara."

"I love you, too."

She hung up the phone and thanked God for blessing her with such an awesome mate. How many men would do all that he did not only for her and their children but for her mother as well. So much for the evil in-law theory.

*Homeward bound.*

# Chapter Eleven

# 2 p.m.

After she saw Lily out for the day, Rose sat down in her rocker and once again began pressing all of the buttons on the remote control thingamajigs. She smiled thinking, *Anybody who saw me doing this might think I was doing an impression of Ray Charles playing the piano—tickling every button on every one of them.* Steve had asked her several times if she wanted him to put a sticker on the one that turns on the TV.

"What on earth would make you think I needed that?" she asked him. He said, "Oh, nothing." Now she kind of wished that she hadn't been so prideful. *What's so wrong with just admitting that you don't know how to do something?*

Finally, by process of elimination, she hit the power button and the TV came on. They had 400 and some odd channels, and all any of them could ever say was, "There's nothing on TV." Nothing *worth watching* is what they meant. And it was true.

Rose marveled at how TV had become such a staple in people's lives. There was no such thing as TV when she was a little girl. They would huddle around the old wooden console radio and listen to the weekly episodes of *The Lone*

*Ranger* and *Little Orphan Annie*. The rest of the time they were too busy for passive entertainment.

The kids had their chores to do, but they never really seemed like work. They didn't have video games and all the electronic gadgetry kids today have, so they had to make up their own games to get their chores done. One of Rose's favorites was "ice skater," in which they would put towels on their feet and skate across the floor to buff it. When the table needed to be set they would turn it into a race and see who could put the dishes, silverware, and napkins out fastest. Of course, that was back when tables were set properly with the silverware in the right places and when the napkins were real, not paper. Nowadays the only time a table got set even close to formally was on holidays.

Even when the girls were young Rose had the table set every night. It made the nightly experience of eating dinner a special occasion instead of something you do in your car after speaking into a blaring metal box. Food came off of the stove and out of the oven and not out of fast food paper bags or cardboard boxes. Families sat together at the table, not in front of the TV.

The girls loved to help Rose make dinner. It really was like a 1950s TV show. When Jack arrived home they would run to door and greet him with hugs and kisses. Carol always wanted to hang up his coat, and then she and Sara would lead him to his seat at the head of the table. They would brag about what they had done to assist in the preparation of the meal. Jack would say the blessing and would always compliment the meal at least a half dozen times in order to cover all of the things the girls had helped with.

No one left the table without taking her plate into the kitchen and everyone helped wash the dishes in assembly-line fashion. There was no dishwasher back then. That came as a surprise from Jack on their 20th wedding anniversary— along with a beautiful pair of pearl earrings. He said, "Now, my Rose, we can spend more time having fun after dinner and less time dealing with dishes."

And they did have fun after dinner every night for almost 35 more years.

She had landed on a news channel—and all they were doing was arguing, and arguing didn't make bad news any better. She shut the TV off, realizing it had taken her longer to figure out how to turn the TV on and back off again than it did to figure out that there was nothing on that she really wanted to watch.

Maybe she could pass a little time reading the large-print romance novel Sara had picked up for her. She used to love to read, and romance novels were her favorite because she was truly a hopeless romantic. Good thing her husband had been, too.

She opened the book and held it close, then held it at arms' length and thought, *You know you're getting on up there when large print is too small to read and your tri-focals are thick as pop bottles.* She looked around for her magnifying glass but couldn't locate it. Stir crazy—it was time to stir around a little. She went to her bedroom and put on a sweater then went back out onto the front porch. It was almost time for school to let out, so maybe she would see a little action out there—some signs of life, maybe a passing car or school bus, a jogger, some children riding bikes.

It was cool and crisp on the porch. Good thing Sara wasn't there; she would scold her for trying to catch pneumonia. The sun was warm between the gusts of the breeze. She was hardy enough yet for an Autumn day.

A passing neighbor honked the horn and waved. Rose nodded in reply, didn't feel like waving. *Haven't I become an old curmudgeon?* She used to be such a social butterfly. She and Jack were always close with their neighbors. Their kids all grew up together. They passed from first grade through high school together, were in the same Sunday School class, attended the same teen camp. The parents were all in PTA together and volunteered for field trips and camp-outs together.

A sudden change in the breeze carried along the bittersweet scent of those rust and yellow chrysanthemums and it reminded her of the first trip she and Jack took to California to visit Carol and Bill. They thought it would be fun to get away for a month. They were empty-nesters, mostly retired at the time, so they packed their bags and headed for the west coast and had a grand time, leaving no stone on the Pacific Coast Highway unturned.

Most of their friends had struggled to adjust after their children left home. Not Jack and Rose. They relished their time together, having learned early on in their marriage that they needed "alone time" together without the children or other couples. When the weather was nice they would spend their alone time in the garden. During the winter months they would take time to be alone together after the girls went to bed. Sometimes Jack would put on his Frank Sinatra albums and sing every song to Rose. She always suspected that he secretly wanted to be part of the Rat Pack.

Then they would talk. After addressing the family or household issues of the day, Jack would pose a question for them to ponder, such as: "If you could move to any planet in the universe, which one would it be and why?" or "If you were crowned Queen, what rules would you make for your kingdom?" or "What do you think heaven will be like and who would you like to see first when you get there...and why?"

Jack would answer the *heaven question*—a perennial favorite—with "Jesus, of course," but then later he added Elvis to the list. Then, after they lost their parents, the answers became more heartfelt and occasionally tearful as they shared their memories of those who had passed.

The answer to the *heaven question* was easy enough for Rose now: Jack. Her Jack. St. Peter would show her in to Jesus, who would show her in to Jack—and there he would be, in his glory, memory restored, fully whole and alive, just as he was as a man of 40, only better.

They had company in the empty nest for three-and-a-half years. After Jack's mother passed away, Jack's father, Cecil, came to live with them. They moved Cecil into Sara's room. He never "cramped their style," as they say—*not the way*, Rose thought, *I am cramping poor Sara's style.* Cecil was a quiet man and preferred to keep to himself and would spend weeks at a time with his daughter, Therese, Jack's sister.

They traveled a lot during their empty-nest years. Besides California, they would go out to Las Vegas once a year, up to Canada, down to Florida, and were fond of taking weekend trips to Door County, Wisconsin, where they would stay in a quaint Bed and Breakfast. They never stay away long. Their home had always been their haven.

After Cecil went to spend the last years of his life with Jack's younger sister Gloria in Montana, Jack and Rose decided to do some remodeling. Carol's bedroom became their exercise room. They outfitted it with a weight bench, a treadmill, and a new stereo system to listen to music while they exercised.

They turned Sara's room into a relaxation room. They put in a loveseat and divan, some softer lighting, and dozens of candles. The music in there was always soft and soothing. They would spend a little time each evening sitting in the flickering glow of the candles—not saying much, just holding hands and being together.

They completely renovated the backyard, adding a gazebo off the patio and a lighted brick walkway to the garden. Jack built up the flower beds so Rose wouldn't have to bend as much, but most days he found her on her knees adding another flower to the garden or mixing plant food into the soil.

From day one, they made a pact that 117 Mitchell would be a place of peace and happiness. When they had a disagreement they would take it away from the house—by taking a walk or a drive to the local coffee shop to talk through the issue. They didn't always agree, but they always stood together on whatever decision they agreed on.

*If their relationship had not been so heavenly good for those 55 years, those last five years wouldn't have been so hellishly bad.*

Alzheimer's changed everything. It began harmlessly enough. Jack would forget where he put his keys and wallet. Then he, who had always been such an eloquent man with a huge vocabulary, began having problems finding the right word to express his thoughts. How frustrated he would become. "Listen to me," he would say, "I sound like some blubbering idiot. What's the word?"

Rose couldn't help but cry as she recalled how devastating it was for Jack to realize that day by day his intelligence was seeping away. The day he was diagnosed with Alzheimer's disease was as dark as any day after. Jack didn't say a word on the way home. He who had always been able to make the glass half full knew with Alzheimer's it was no use. So he sat there stone-cold silent. He spent the afternoon sitting out in the garden. There was nothing to say.

They went to one specialist after another hoping against hope that they would get a different answer. They didn't. Jack spent hours every day trying to figure out how to keep his brain active. He ordered Harry Lorayne's memory course and worked crossword puzzles and word searches. He took one medication after another, and the better ones kept him stable for a while, but the disease eventually won over the medicine.

Then came the angry outbursts that left Rose reeling. Jack was the most even-tempered man she had ever known. When he was upset he would go for a walk to talk it out or let off steam, but the disease had stripped him of his ability to cope. She had never seen her *gentle Jack* so much as lose his cool. Now he was prone to fits of rage. She would do her best to get him calmed down. The Frank Sinatra albums worked sometimes; he could sing those old songs even after he lost his memory of his daughters' names. When he was in the early stages of the disease Rose would often find him sitting out in the garden with the Frank Sinatra music blaring out of the windows. She would go out and sit with him.

He would say: "Let me look at you, Rose. I don't want to forget your face."

"What if I forget the girls?"

"I don't want to forget my girls. They are my angels."

"Do you think I'll remember the garden?"

"Just know this: I will always remember you in my heart."

How agonizing it was as she watched as his soul—the person she had fallen in love with and spent over 50 years with—passed away before her very eyes. Then there was nothing left but his body. Near the end, it was like going to an open-casket wake every day. She would sit bedside wishing God would take him home and make him whole while at the same time wanting him ever to be there so she could go on holding his hand without end. Even though he hardly recognized her at all during that last year, his eyes still sparkled just a little when she would hold his hand.

His hands were so frail she was afraid she might break a bone if she squeezed too hard. Often, as if by instinct, he would hold her hand back, just as if they were sitting out in the garden at 117 Mitchell Place. For hours on end they would sit there with the songs of Frank Sinatra playing softly in the background.

Sara didn't come often—usually only when Rose would play on her guilt. Then she would come on Jack's birthday or for a drive-by visit during the holidays. She couldn't seem to get it over with soon enough. She would say, "Mother, what difference does it make? He doesn't even know who I am. I will be just one more stranger in the room."

"It might make more of a difference than you think, Sara," Rose would tell her. "Even if he doesn't remember who we are, he will at least know that somebody loves him."

He would have "episodes" nearly every day, usually when the time came time to get him bathed and dressed for the day. He—whom Rose had never heard utter the word "damn"—would let go a barrage of shocking profanity. Rose didn't even know Jack knew such nasty words. The staff took it in stride. They gave Rose pamphlets on the disease to try to help her understand. To them he was a patient showing symptoms of a disease; to her, he was the man with whom she had spent every day for over half a century.

Sara couldn't bear seeing her father, whom she still referred to as Daddy, cussing and carrying on in that manner. He had never raised his voice to the girls. Sara said, "Mother, I just cannot bear to see him like this, and I don't want his grandchildren to remember their grandfather like this."

She wouldn't even ask about him when she would talk to Rose during the week—as if he didn't exist. When Rose would try to tell Sara about him, she would politely listen and then excuse herself from the conversation or say that something had just come up and she would have to call Rose back later.

It was all so much easier for Carol, of course. She only came back home a few times that last year. She would see her father several times for an hour or so, then fly back home to California to her real life. Then she called once a week, asked all of the right questions, listened to all of the answers, and then hung up and went back to her real life.

*Rose knew it was hard on the girls, but did they ever really stop and consider how hard it was on her sitting there day by day by day?*

She scanned her eyes over Sara and Steve's yard. Maybe she could do some gardening, pull some weeds or edge the raised garden beds. Sara and Steve didn't have time to fool with the yard. In the summer Sara had a landscaping service come out, but they didn't really care. They were hired guns and Rose knew they took down more flowers than weeds with their high-powered weed whacker.

For years, Rose and Jack had come over during week-days when Sara and Steve were working and tended the flower beds. It felt good doing something to help their career-woman daughter (Jack was *so* proud of Sara), but after Jack got sick he just didn't have the time or energy to do it anymore. It was all she could do to come home and do her own gardening. But she did it, because that was hallowed ground for her and Jack. The garden was a sacred shrine to their life together.

The garden was the one place where she could still feel close to him. How hard it was to watch it become overgrown after her fall. She remembered sitting on the garden bench crying, her legs scratched from the overgrown brush, as she surveyed the wilted roses and the thorns tangled in the vines on the trellis and choking the color from the flower blossoms, leaving the garden strangled and lifeless.

*Well maybe I can do a little something for Sara's garden,* she thought, as she made her way out of the porch rocker and down the front steps. She was always a little nervous on the uneven ground—not nervous enough to use a cane or walker, however, which is what Sara wanted.

*It was bad enough knowing you're an old woman without showing that you're one!*

She made her way to the edge of the landscape for a closer look. In Autumn it was hard to tell the weeds from the flowers. She began to pull the weeds around the mums that were in full bloom. *These kids,* she thought, *never even stop to appreciate the beauty of these mums!*

*Kids! I'm talking about people in their 50s as though they are schoolchildren. They are adults with adult jobs and kids of their own, who really aren't even kids themselves anymore. Their kids are in their 20s. Where did the time go? And how did I get so old?*

After 10 minutes or so of pulling weeds and moving the dirt around, Rose was getting a little tired. *It must be those pain pills,* she decided. Maybe she should head back inside and rest a while.

Once in her room she tuned the radio to KLOVE 94.3. She usually listened to radio preachers during the day, but today she was in the mood for a little music—young people's music. KLOVE played more contemporary gospel music than the AM station she usually listened to. A promotion came on for a Christian music festival that was coming to the area in a few weeks.

*Wouldn't that be fun!* she thought.

Back when the girls were young, gospel festivals were a favorite family outing. They would load up a picnic basket, grab a blanket, and head off to the fest. Those were such special times. Maybe she would see if Sara and Steve might want to go. She decided to ask them about it at dinner. She took off her glasses and lay down on the bed and closed her eyes and listened to the words of the song that was playing.

The lyrics were about showing those around you how much you love them. There were times recently, she had to admit, when she was so preoccupied with getting others—mainly Sara—to meet her needs that she was not very loving or considerate of their needs.

Before her fall and rehab, she was always on the giving end of love and care. She had always tried to be there for her family, and now here she was having to depend on them.

*Poor Sara.* She had taken the brunt of it. *They say the ones you love the most are the ones you can hurt—and be hurt by—most, and lately that had certainly been the case.* She lay there and thought about how close she and her "baby" daughter Sara had always been. There was nothing they couldn't share. Now it was as if there was a Great Wall of Resentment between them.

She wondered for the first time what it must really be like to be in Sara's shoes. It wasn't as if she just woke up one day and said, "Gee, I think I'd like Mom to have to come live with us—and be an invalid—and destroy our empty nest so we won't have any time for golf or dancing lessons or even a walk around the block in the evenings."

She had always thought she knew what it was like to have company in the empty nest. But Cecil was a whole different story. First off, Rose had a part-time job and could pretty much come and go as she pleased, which enabled her to run whatever errands she needed to run before Jack got home in the evening. She didn't have a career like Sara, and a very demanding career at that. Cecil was much younger than Rose when he came to live with them and in pretty good health, and he was a private man who enjoyed being left to himself most of the time. By contrast, Rose thought, *I'm a broken down old lady who needs so much done for her. And of all the things I love, being alone is not one of them.* So when poor Sara and Steve got home in the evening, there was Rose ready to talk about the day—when they were pretty well talked out.

Then there was the fact that Cecil had two other children, one who lived within 100 miles. So Cecil would rarely be with Jack and Rose for more than a month at a stretch without going to spend a week or two with one of his daughters.

"Dear Lord," Rose prayed aloud, "please help me to be less of a burden to my daughter, or just take me home whenever you're ready, so I can be with my Jack. Help me show

Sara how much I love and appreciate all that she has done for me and the sacrifices she has made for me. Heal our relationship, please. In Jesus' name, Amen."

She sat there thinking what she could do that might ease Sara's burden. She might have dozed off for a few minutes because when she came to the house was dark. At least there was the glow from the TV to light the room.

*Oh, Rose,* she thought, *you did it again.* She forgot where the light switch was. She would be sitting watching TV waiting for Sara and Steve to get home, and before she knew it the sun had set and it was dark outside and therefore dark inside the house. Her eyes were not what they used to be, so she would shuffle around for a little bit trying to figure out where the switch was, but after a few minutes her fear of falling would lead her to shuffle right back to the couch and wait it out until somebody came home. It was so embarrassing. It was no problem in the long days of summer, but the days were getting shorter…and so was her memory.

It must be frustrating for Sara to come home so often to a dark house, knowing that her mother was too far gone to figure out how to turn the lights on. The first few times it happened, Sara had apologized, as if it were her fault that the lights were off, and this made Rose even more humiliated.

She sat there in the blue glow of the TV and resolved: I will do what I can to ease Sara's burden. I will….

# Chapter Twelve

# 6 p.m.

By the time Sara pulled into the driveway it was a little before 6:00 and deep into dusk. The house was dark—again. There was nothing worse than coming home and finding her mother waiting for her in the dark. It was never a good sign. Sara got a feeling in the pit of her stomach every time she saw the dark house, she knew she would walk in and find her mother sitting in the living room stewing over something. *What did I do this time?*

She opened the garage door with the remote and pulled in, wishing that Steve was already home. Since he was picking up dinner at Provino's he would be at least 15 minutes behind her. Those first few minutes after getting home were always so tense and awkward. She shut the car off and sat there for a moment in the dark dreading going into her own home.

To come home from a long day—especially a day as long and trying as today had been—and have her mom sitting there alone and silent in the darkness stewing on the injustice of it all was just a little too much. Sara couldn't help it that she had to work dawn to dark. They had tried leaving the porch light burning all day, but somehow it always managed to get turned off during the day.

Sara walked in and flipped on the hallway light then made her way in to the kitchen and turned on the overhead light, then the stove light then switched on the living room light.

"Hi, Mom," she called out as she quickly moved past her mother and headed for the stairs.

"Hello, Sara," she said, "how was your day?"

Sara let her purse drop on the floor. The clunk might have been her jaw. *How was my day? Did I come into the wrong house? This is 2509 Brookhollow Drive, isn't it?* She tried to remember the last time her mother had asked her how she was doing....

"Okay," she said, her voice faltering. "I'm going to go up and change clothes." She was already halfway up the stairs when she said, "Steve will be home in a few minutes with dinner so I'll be down in a jiffy."

"Take your time, Sara," she heard her mother's voice say.

*Take my time? Who was that woman sitting in the rocker in my living room? What have they done with my mother?*

She changed into a pair of jeans, a sweatshirt, and her fuzzy pink slippers and went down to the kitchen where she found her mother, of all things, setting the table, all the while humming the tune to a new song they played on KLOVE. *That's weird? Mom doesn't listen to that "contemporary" music. She prefers gospel music written before the turn of the century—the 19th century at that.*

Sara said, "What are you doing, Mother?"

"Setting the table."

"I can see that."

"Then why'd you ask?" her mother said.

*Very funny.* "Because, well, I mean, what are you doing?"

"Just trying to help out a little. No sense being old *and* useless."

"Uh...." Before Sara had a chance to say whatever it was she was going to say—probably something a little sarcastic like: *Who are you and what are you doing in my house?*—the door opened and in walked Steve with a bag of food in each arm.

"Hello, ladies," he said in that charming singsong tone. "How are my two favorite gals tonight?" He headed over and set the bags down on the counter. He gave Sara a kiss then went to the table and planted a peck on Rose's cheek.

"Did Sara tell you the wonderful news, Mom?"

"Why no," she said, and Sara winced, thinking she was going to say something on the order of *Why would she talk to me?* But she only said, "Sara just got home a minute or two ago and we haven't had a chance to talk. So what's the wonderful news?"

"Well," Steve said, "I—"

"He got the contract," Sara told her. And the way it came out was a little flat even to her own ear.

"Oh, Steve, that's just wonderful," her mother said. "Well, good for you. I knew you could do it!"

Sara thought, You *knew he could do it...and* I, *his wife, don't even know what IT is....*

"Thank you, my favorite mother-in-law. Sounds like you were a little more confident about it than I was. It turned out a lot better than I hoped. They signed a two-year exclusive with us, which is almost unheard of these days. You know how tough it is to get a 30-day commitment these days."

"I'm sure I don't have any idea how you two do all you do," her mother said. "I never had anything but a part-time job."

Sara set the pans of lasagna and ziti on the table and thought—*Did I just hear mother include me in something that was pretty close to a compliment?*

Her mother was getting the napkins off the counter. *And she's helping out?*

Rose said, "But I can say that I never doubted that you could do anything you set your mind to. Jack always said, 'Steve Chapin might be the smartest man I've ever met.'"

"Well, that made my night, Mom," Steve told her. "My head will be so big I won't be able to get through the door if you keep that up."

"Isn't it wonderful, Sara?"

"Yes, Mother." She could feel herself becoming annoyed. *Why do I feel like the odd man out? Did anybody care that she was trying just to get through what might rank in the Top 10 of the worst days of her life? Did they care? Did anyone ask?*

*Actually, Mom did when I first got home. But did she really care? What's come over her?*

During dinner, Steve shared all the exciting details of his high-powered pow-wow. The president of the client company was *very impressed*, he said. All Sara could think of was how disappointed the president of *her* company, Stan Westin, had been over her gaffe.

Sara watched Steve's face as he spoke. He was so animated. He hadn't really had a lot to celebrate lately. In the two years since he had resigned his post in Corporate America to found his own IT consulting start-up things hadn't gone as well as he had hoped. He needed a win. And finally he got one, and there she was, his devoted wife, drinking the bitter wine of sour grapes.

*He was riding so high on the overdue success...so why did that make her want to smack somebody?*

There was a glint in his eye and a lilt in his voice and not a boring bone in his body. And it was all of those things — and more — that had first drawn her to him almost three decades ago. He was so animated, like some fun-loving sitcom character who had an amusing anecdote and word of encouragement for everyone he met.

She remembered how he approached her from across the lecture hall on the first day of college in their freshman chemistry class. His pick-up line was, "Want to blow something up together?" and it worked.

She even recalled how he looked that day, his wavy brown hair tousled from the wind and his bright green eyes sparkling like emeralds when he told a story. He had on faded Levi's and an I © NY t-shirt, which was ironic considering that he had never even been to New York. He admitted that he had gotten the shirt at a garage sale at his neighbor's house before he left for school. They became fast friends, and by their sophomore year they were inseparable.

It was *fun at first sight* and maybe even love at first sight. After that first class together they went out for lunch that lasted three hours and ended only because she had another class to get to that afternoon.

She enjoyed being around Steve from the pick-up line on. They seemed to mesh from the very beginning. When she got out of her afternoon class that first day Steve was waiting for her on a bench outside the classroom building. He acted surprised to see her and said that he had found that this particular bench seemed to have some magical powers— namely, it could make him irresistible to women. Sara had laughed at that, thinking: *I believe in magic.*

They would talk for hours on end. She never tired of being around him. All through college, her friends questioned why she didn't "play the field" and date other men to be sure he was The One.

He was.

Between bites of ziti she glanced over at her mother, who was listening intently to every word Steve spoke. She was nodding and oohing and aahing and probing for details about the meeting. Steve had always loved an audience, and Sara had always thought he should go into acting instead of computers.

Her mother was carrying on like a Plain Jane schoolgirl who got the undivided attention of the star quarterback of the football team. Sara smiled at the thought. Sara wondered if her mom had a secret crush on Steve. He listened to her, shared stories with her, paid attention to her. *Who wouldn't have a crush on him?*

After they finished eating, Sara stood up and picked up her plate, and reached for her mother's, but Weird made another appearance: Her mother raised her hand in a *halt* gesture, cocked her head, and said, "Thank you, dear, but I think I'm still able to get my own plate to the sink."

Steve went right on talking, so Sara said, "Are you sure?" Her mother merely nodded and smiled, and Sara picked up her laptop and headed into the living room for a little mindless TV time. She wasn't sure what was on and really didn't care; she just needed something to distract her. She wanted to get a head start on some memos for her staff and put together an outline of her notes from the day's meeting. She thought she better be ahead of the game tomorrow after dropping the ball today.

Job one was to make a list of all of the projects she could delegate to Jane and the other members of her staff. Under each project title she made bullet points listing all tasks associated with the project so that there would be no misunderstanding. She also made a list of resources needed for each project.

As she banged away at the keyboard she could hear her mother and Steve still sitting at the kitchen table talking. For just a moment, she thought about getting up and going into the kitchen to join them. There was a part of her that wanted to; it seemed as if they were enjoying their time together. She thought about her conversation with Heidy…. But there was just so much that she had to do before tomorrow and she was already comfortable—more or less.

She muted the TV and eavesdropped.

"Oh, Steve, you must have been so excited when they signed that contract. Were you nervous? And to think, I almost made you late this morning chatting over coffee."

"Nonsense," Steve said. "I was so engrossed in our chat I lost track of the time. I had forgotten about Jack's Dad coming to live with you. That would have been when Sara and I were in college."

"Sara loved her Grandpa Barnes, let me tell you."

Steve seemed to have the kind of easy relationship with her mother that Sara used to have....

"By the way, how did your therapy go today? You seemed to be in some pain this morning."

"That," her mother said, with the throaty little laugh that had been as comforting to Sara as a warm sweater throughout her life. "Well, I was feeling sorry for myself and called and canceled the appointment. I should have gone. It wouldn't have been so bad. I owe it to myself and to you and Sara to get along as best I can. It wasn't the worst pain I've ever had to endure."

*Well, what on earth?*

Steve said, "I broke my wrist when I was in my glory years: Pop Warner football league. I was nine at the time. The wrist healed just fine, but ever since I have had a throbbing pain in my arm. I can't even imagine what a hip fracture would feel like...."

Sara could hear how genuine his concern was for her mom. And a flash of anger burned in her gut. *I'm the one who has to deal with all her pain issues and the tantrums when she didn't want to go to therapy. I was the one who had to deal with the phone call from Sister Carol the Saint and now Steve gets to be the hero. Mr. Wonderful, all concerned about Rose. It just didn't seem fair.*

"So I played hooky and sat out on the porch like some old woman."

"Oh, Mom," he said, "you're just a spring chicken yet."

"I feel more like a *plucked* chicken most days." They both laughed.

*Sara had heard just about enough out of the mutual admiration club!*

She tried to bring her mind back to her work, but she had become so irritated listening to them. She banged on the laptop keys, occasionally looking up to see what was on television. She un-muted it to drown out the sickly sweet conversation in the kitchen and turned her attention back to her work. She tried to make a mental list of the things she thought she could get accomplished before bedtime.

It was strange, she thought, how her mother could be so different with Steve than she was with Sara. Her mother was so short with her, but let Steve walk into the room, and she was just as sweet as could be. She heard Steve get up from the table and open one of the kitchen drawers.

"Okay, Rose, name your poison—dice or rummy?"

"I think I'd rather beat you at rummy tonight. You're not much of a challenge at dice lately."

"Well Rose, if I didn't know you better, I'd swear I just heard you 'trash-talk' me. Rummy it is, and you better have your nickels ready because I'll show you no mercy." They both laughed.

She could hear the whirring sound of the deck of cards as Steve did his "magic" shuffle. With half the deck in each hand he would fan them from one hand to the other as if they cards were stuck together like a Slinky.

"That's all window-dressing," Rose told him. "Too bad your fancy shuffling can't help your game, mister!"

"We'll see about that," Steve said. Then: "Hey, Sara, why don't you turn off the computer and come join us for a friendly game of rummy? That way I can beat you and Mom at the same time."

"Come on and have a little fun with us, Sara," her mother added. "I have a change purse full of nickels to cover you, and I'll even put a bag of popcorn in the microwave."

Sara sat thought about it for a moment before opting to continue with business over pleasure. "No thanks, not tonight."

"Come on, honey. It's not every day Mom offers to burn—ahem, *make*—us some popcorn. Come play with us."

"I'll have to pass, thank you," Sara said as politely as she could. "I have a lot to get done before tomorrow."

"Be that way, then," Steve said. "But you're going to miss witnessing the greatest defeat in rummy history."

"I'll have to settle for pictures and a t-shirt," she said. "Maybe next time."

"Okay, but it's your loss," her husband replied.

"No," her mother said, "it'll be *your* loss, Steve."

"Let the games begin," Steve said."

Sara tried to concentrate on her work. Why couldn't she just get up and go in and enjoy a game of cards with her husband and mother? It was almost as if doing so would be an admission of something...as if by staying in the living room working she was saving face....

# Chapter Thirteen

# 6 p.m.

Rose heard the garage door open.She was relieved that someone was finally home.She had been sitting in the dark for a short time but it was frustrating.At least there was the glow from the TV to give a little light to the room.

*It was so embarrassing, she thought. How could I let this happen so often?*

Each time she would think that she should make herself a note to remind her to put the lights on around four o'clock each afternoon so that when it got dark they would already be on.In the summer this wasn't an issue since it didn't get dark until later and by then someone was always home.However, it was if the shortened days in the fall and winter time took her by surprise.

She heard the door leading from the garage to the house open.She wanted to call out a greeting but was too mortified by her predicament to say anything.*They must think that I am a feeble old woman.*

It must be frustrating for Sara to come home so often to a dark house, knowing that her mother is too dim-witted to figure out how to turn the lights on.

When it first started happening, Sara would apologize as if it were her fault that the lights were off, this made Rose even more humiliated. After it became a all too regular scene, Rose figured that Sara must have sensed her shame at her inability to find the switch and out of respect would just turn on the lights and head upstairs to change her clothes.

"Hi, Mom," Sara said.

"Hello, Sara," Rose said, and trying to break through the awkwardness added, "how was your day?"

Rose eased up out of her rocker and shuffled into the kitchen. The least she could do was set the table. Sara had had a long day at work and was probably tired. In her day, Rose was a pretty good cook—up until the day she fell and broke her hip. She had done little more than heated a can of tomato soup since. Every once in a while Sara would make dumplings or spaghetti sauce from Rose's own recipe. She thought maybe one day next week she might ask Lily to help her make a meatloaf and creamed potatoes and surprise Sara and Steve.

Sara dropped her purse, said, "Okay," then went upstairs to change her clothes. She called back down: "Steve will be home in a few minutes with dinner, so I'll be down in a jiffy."

"Take your time, Sara," she said.

Rose began setting the table. She was arranging the silverware and singing that contemporary song she had heard on KLOVE—she was of a mind to buy that record—when Sara came down in her jeans and sweatshirt.

"What are you doing?" *Sara seems confused, I know it's been a while but I have set the table before.*

"Setting the table."

"I can see that," Sara said.

"Then why'd you ask?" Rose said. She smiled, thinking that Sara, who had always enjoyed being on the giving end of sarcasm, might enjoy that. Then, judging from the way Sara rolled her eyes, Rose thought: *I hope I haven't spoiled the evening trying to be clever.*

"Because, well, I mean, what are you doing?"

"Just trying to help out a little," Rose told her trying to hide the embarrassment she felt. "No sense being old *and* useless."

Sara just stood there, saying, "Uh...."

*Maybe she's just surprised—pleasantly—that I'm actually doing something besides waiting around to be catered to.*

In came Steve with a sack of food in each hand. "Hello, ladies," he said. "How are my two favorite gals tonight?" He headed towards the stove and gave Sara a kiss and then to the table to give Rose a peck on the cheek.

"Did Sara tell you the wonderful news, Mom?"

"Why no," she told him. She was thinking, *I wish Sara would share any news with me.* But, really, Rose had to admit, she was so negative most of the time—talking about this ache or that pain—that poor Sara didn't want to have to listen to that after getting home from a stressful day at the office. *Who would?* She said, "Sara just got home a minute or two ago and we haven't had a chance to talk. So what's the wonderful news?"

"Well," Steve said, "I—"

"He got the contract," Sara told her. She didn't sound too excited about. If that had been Jack who just landed that big contract Rose would have been as giddy as a schoolgirl and wouldn't expect him to stop and pick up dinner, either. She would have prepared his favorite dinner—beef pot roast with baby carrots and a burgundy-mushroom gravy—and had Sinatra crooning softly through the house when he got home....

*There now. Enough of that. Sara is not you, Rose. And this is a whole different world. Sara works very hard and she is stressed. No good can come of constantly judging your daughter by your own standards.*

"Oh, Steve, that's just wonderful," Rose told him. "Well, good for you. I knew you could do it!"

"Thank you, my favorite mother-in-law," he said, winking those pretty green eyes at her. "Sounds like you were a little more confident about it than I was. It turned out a lot better than I hoped. They signed a two-year exclusive with us, which is almost unheard of these days. You know how tough it is to get a 30-day commitment these days."

"I'm sure I don't have any idea how you two do all you do," she said, making sure to include Sara. For it was Sara who had been the primary bread-winner for the family since Steve left his job to go to work for himself. "I never had anything but a part-time job."

A part-time job that she enjoyed to the extent that it gave her a little pocket change to do something special for Jack and the girls and didn't intrude on her time "making the home," as they say. One thing she especially enjoyed about her job, however, was negotiating with the vendors from around the world. Their asking price was just that, and if you didn't dicker they were leery of doing business with you.

She recalled the day Sara called and told her that Steve had decided to leave his corporate job and start his own consulting firm. Rose tried her best to be supportive, but she was a little concerned. Not that she didn't have a lot of faith in and respect for Steve—she surely did—but she knew that it would put more pressure on Sara.

What concerned Rose now was that Sara was not more excited about Steve's big news. She hardly seemed interested. *Is she depressed or merely stressed out?* Rose wondered. All her days lately seemed to be long and hard.

As she listened to Steve recount the details of the meeting, she thought how much he reminded her of Jack. Sara had chosen a man just like her father—and what a wonderful choice it was. Steve and Jack were both bright, articulate, outgoing, and fun to be around. Sometimes being around

Steve made Rose not so lonely for Jack; sometimes it made her miss him more.

Rose wasn't surprised when Sara got up immediately after dinner. She wasn't one to sit around and chat. She picked up her own plate and started to pick up Rose's, but Rose put up her hand and said, "Thank you, dear, but I think I'm still able to get my own plate to the sink."

From the look on Sara's face, Rose might have just said that had decided to run the Chicago Marathon! She said, "Are you sure, Mother?"

Then Sara went into the living room, as she did every night as soon as she finished eating. Steve would stay with Rose at the table and talk about his work or her therapy but mainly about how things were "back in the day." He just didn't seem to be able to get enough information about what things were like with Jack and Rose at this or that stage of their life.

He was always so kind to her; she was concerned at times that she was repeating herself.Rose had heard friends at the Senior Center jokingly refer to it as "Sometimers disease." If she did, he never let on. He would just sit there drinking his after-dinner coffee and wink and nod and ask questions. It had gotten to the point where she would start every story with, "I might have told you this before, but...." Just in case.

Yet it was sweet the way he allowed her to reminisce. He was a good man and she thanked God every day for bringing him to her daughter, just as every day she hoped Sara would stay and talk with them. She missed the way they used to be, so easy and free with each other. But each night Sara retreated to the living room with her computer so she could get back to work—as if her life were really intruding on her work. *Wasn't that opposite the way it was supposed to be?*

As if she hadn't done enough in her 10-hour day at the office. Rose knew that Sara had an assistant and other support staff, yet every night she came home with work. It seemed unfair that her boss would put that much pressure on one person. Though, knowing her daughter, Sara probably took a lot of it on herself. Still, she never stopped hoping that Sara would join them if only for a half a cup of coffee and a few minutes of light talk.

Rose turned her attention to Steve.

Then Steve asked about her therapy and whether it had helped with the pain. Rose had tried her best to hide the intensity of her pain that morning. She really didn't want either of them fussing over her. She was feeling better and didn't want to worry him. She knew, too, that the issue of her canceling the therapy appointment was a "sore spot" with Sara.

She raised her voice a notch, "Well, I was feeling sorry for myself and called and canceled the appointment. I should have gone. It wouldn't have been so bad. I owe it to myself and to you and Sara to get along as best I can. It wasn't the worst pain I've ever had to endure."

Rose heard Sara turn up the TV in the living room.She knew Sara was pretty engrossed in her work so she could only hope that she heard her.Steve was saying something about his wrist. Rose prayed silently: "Please dear Lord, help Sara. I'm so worried about her health. Give her peace of mind, body, and soul, please. In Jesus' name, Amen."

Then Steve challenged her to a game of dice or rummy. Steve was so lighthearted and fun when it came to games. As for Sara, well, she just wanted to win. She was always so serious about games, even as a small child she would throw a tantrum if someone else won. Rose and Jack worried about her reaction and tried to explain that winning wasn't everything, and Sara said, "But losing is NOTHING!" Well, Rose thought, I guess that competitive nature had served her well in the business world.

Rose whispered, "Why don't you see if Sara wants to join us, Steve? She really needs to take a break and have a little fun."

"I don't know, Mom," he said. "You know how my wife is when she is working. I'm not sure I can drag her away from that computer. I actually was thinking of surgically attaching the computer to her so it would be more convenient." He smiled but not because he thought it was funny.

He spoke up, so as to be heard over the blaring TV: "Okay, Rose, name your poison—dice or rummy?"

He did his "magic shuffle" and they exchanged some bantering game-talk. Then she nodded in the direction of the living room and winked at Steve, who said, "Hey, Sara, why don't you turn off the computer and come join us for a friendly game of rummy? That way I can beat you and Mom at the same time."

There was no answer, so Rose added: "Come on and have a little fun with us, Sara. have a change purse full of nickels to cover you and I'll even put a bag of popcorn in the microwave."

"No thanks, not tonight."

"Come on, honey," Steve pleaded. "It's not every day Mom offers to burn—ahem *make*—us some popcorn. Come play with us."

"I'll have to pass, thank you," Sara told them. "I have a lot to get done before tomorrow."

*No dice...and no rummy.*

Rose craned her neck and peeked in at her daughter in the living room. She could just make out Sara's silhouette hunched over the computer, hands pounding away at the keys. Rose and Steve exchanged sad nods. Steve shrugged.

Rose heard the volume on the TV go up again. It was obvious that Sara was trying to drown out the fun and games in the kitchen.

# Chapter Fourteen

# 8 p.m.

Sara wanted to make sure she got to bed early. She needed to be at her desk no later than 7 a.m. to get a jump on her day. She really needed to make a dent in that mountain of stuff in her inbox. She thought about calling it a night and turning off the computer and heading up to bed. In the kitchen the fun and games went on. They had been at their game of rummy for over an hour now.

Sara looked up again at the muted TV and her eye fixed on an 8x10 picture on the mantelpiece. It was taken at her parent's 50th anniversary party.

She had taken such care in organizing and planning the golden affair as a surprise party. She wanted to make sure every detail was perfect—down to the decorations on the cake. There had never been so many people packed into 117 Mitchell, and they waited with the lights out for the guests of honor to arrive...and they waited...and waited...for two hours past the time they expected Jack and Rose to be back from their celebration dinner at their favorite restaurant, Bambinelli's. Turns out, they had driven over to Hulting Park and reenacted Jack's proposal to Rose in a private ceremony. They had renewed their vows. Once they got home, though, it was quite a celebration, and they partied well into the night.

She scanned the other pictures on the entertainment center—pictures taken on family vacations, at Tommy's graduation, of Sally in her dorm room on her first day of college, of Steve and Sara on their last vacation the autumn before Mom fell.

It was hard to believe it had been over a year since their last vacation. The cruise was a family tradition. They looked forward to it all year, and on January 1 they would even get a big calendar and count down the months, then weeks, then days by crossing off each day with a big red X until.... *Bon Voyage!*

Fall was when they got the best rates, not to mention that they didn't have to contend with raucous spring breakers. They could just sit back and relax for an entire week and let time stand still. No interruptions. No ringing phones. No voicemail. No Blackberry. No e-mails. No worries.

This was the first fall in 10 years that they had not taken a cruise. They had planned to go on an Alaskan cruise, but who had time? What with selling Mom's home and remodeling to accommodate her moving in with them, getting Tommy settled in college, working all that overtime to *justify* her promotion....

What she wouldn't give for just a day or two of vacation from her life—a little downtime away from everything and everyone to relax and do nothing. Every moment of her life was accounted for—from the menial tasks of everyday life to the life-preserving duties of caretaking for her mother. It was as if she were on a treadmill stuck on high speed and no way to slow down.

It was too much, way too much. She needed a break, but there was no way to take that vacation. She couldn't leave her mother at home alone for a week, even with Lily coming daily to check on her. Their days of vacationing—much less cruising—were over until her mother was....

She didn't even want to think about that.

Just the thought of it made her feel guilty. It was so cold. She really didn't want anything to happen to her mother. It was difficult enough losing her father. She couldn't even imagine being without her mom. It wasn't as if she was unrealistic; she knew eventually her mom would die. Everyone has to, eventually. She just didn't want to think about it.

Sara closed her eyes and thought back on her conversation with Heidy. It was a blessing to have a friend who could, as the Bible put it, speak the truth to her in love. There was no doubt that Heidy cared about her. And so she wanted to help Sara look at her situation from a different perspective. The truth was, Sara had been so self-absorbed, so preoccupied with her own needs *and wants* that she had never really looked at the situation from her mother's perspective.

Sure, she would say, "I'm sorry this happened to Mom." That was sympathy, and it was fine as far as it went; it just didn't go very far. Part of the sympathy was always for Sara: *Your fall has completely changed all of our lives!*

Empathy was something totally different. It was the very thing she had tried to engender in her HR staff at Olson. It was a part of effective listening—getting out of your own head and heart and into someone else's.

*If I were in Mom's shoes, what would I be feeling? What would it be like?*

She recalled how difficult it was to watch her mom in the hospital and in the rehabilitation facility. It seemed as though literally overnight her mother had gone from being a very young 80-plus to a very old 80-plus woman. One day she was talking about taking another mission trip to Costa Rica, the next she was lying in the hospital so confused it reminded Sara of her father in the second year of his Alzheimer's.

*If it was hard on me to watch it, how hard must it have been for Mom to go through it, to struggle doing little things like tying her own shoes and taking a shower and finally the sober reality that she would not be returning to 117 Mitchell?*

Then there was the whole sad affair of moving Mom. Sara was so determined to be the strong one—the one mom could always count on. She was so "strong" that she at times had become short-fused and insensitive. One of the reasons she had harbored so much anger at her mother was that her mother seemed so unaffected by the loss of her husband—Sara's father. Then, when her mother did show it, she punished her for it. How many times had she come into her mother's home the week of the move and found her mother sobbing—as inconspicuously as she could—and said, "All right, Mom, we need to get going if we are going to get everything done."

Her mother was going through the sentimental treasures of a lifetime. It was as if a bomb had dropped on her life and now the shards were being packaged up in so many small boxes affixed with a price tag to be sold or given away to strangers. *What if everything that meant anything to me was being sold at auction before my very eyes? Would it be so easy to play the strong one then?*

What if she had to depend on everyone else to help her with the most mundane tasks of daily life? Sara was strong-willed by temperament and had always prided herself on how independent she was. She thought about what it would be like if she had to depend on Sally and Tommy—or even Steve—for everything.

Selling the house was on Sara so she was really focused on the task at hand, stuffing all of her own emotions—after all, it *was* the house that she had grown up in.

All the best memories of her life were centered on 117 Mitchell Place, too, but had she *really* tried to understand what her mom was going through? She tried to convince herself that she had, but deep down she knew she probably hadn't. Not in a Golden Rule sort of way. Not in the way she would want her children to understand if she were her in her mom's place.

How disappointed her mom must have been. There she was selling—*losing*—everything she had and all her daughter could do was make lists and price items. *How had she become so insensitive?* Sara fought back the tears as she turned to look at her mother in the kitchen with Steve.

She had always liked to think of herself as a caring person. In college she had considered majoring in Social Work but then settled on Human Resource Management. She had often joked that, "If you are a helping person who has a strong will you go into HR; if you don't have a strong will, you become a social worker."

At church Sara was on the care team that visited "shut-ins"—those who were confined to their homes due to advanced age or disability—and arranged for them to get the services they needed. She had a gift for connecting with those she visited—her pastor called it "the gift of encouragement"—and could tell that they always felt better after her visits.

*Why do I treat those strangers better than I treat my own mom? The issues she has to deal with are no different from the ones those "shut-ins" have to deal with? And I love my mom. Love is a* verb.

She thought about how many hours she had volunteered helping strangers—doing their shopping for them, helping them write Christmas cards to their friends, and even doing things she detested, such as house-cleaning and laundry. But mostly she just sat and visited with them, empathizing with their situation.

Yet she would become agitated if her own mother called her during the day and asked her to pick up a prescription—and the pharmacy was on the way home!

Heidy was right. Coming to live with them hadn't been Mom's plan all along. In fact, when Sara and Steve first broached the subject of her moving in with them, she initially said, "No! There is no way. The last thing I want is to be a burden to my children."

Rose had even suggested that it would be best for her to move into one of those assisted living communities. Sara and Steve would hear nothing of it. They insisted that she move in with them—and it wasn't an easy sell. Rose was determined. But in the end they prevailed, arguing that it was the best possible arrangement. Steve had a flexible schedule and would be home most days. They would find a personal assistant for her. *Everything would be wonderful.*

In the end, mother had relented. It soon became apparent, however, that they had no idea what it was really like to help care for an aging parent. Sara had no idea just how much of the *burden* would be on her. She did her best to try to keep her mother from sensing her mounting frustration. Yet somehow along the way Sara had lost her connection with her mom and her ability to effectively take care of the people in her life.

She had never felt so lonely in her life. With Sally and Tommy both away in college and Mom there in the house, everything was different. Sara's evening routine was: come home, put together some sort of dinner, sit around the table with her husband and Mom making idle conversation, listen to Mom carry on about her frustrations and complaints, pull out the laptop, watch some mindless TV shows, and go to bed.

Why did she become so annoyed when her mom and Steve would sit at the table after dinner and chat? She never thought of it as jealousy until now. Deep down in her soul that's what it was—her husband was enjoying the close relationship with her mom that she had lost. She would listen in on their conversations and bristle if she felt that they were laughing too much. She hated hearing her mother share stories of her own childhood.

She had become a martyr. She used to go the spa and workout, sit in the sauna and sweat out her stress, get a massage, have dinner with a friend, go on a date with her husband. Take those long walks, just the two of them. After her mother moved in, she stopped. Poor Saint Sara was too busy caring for her pitiful infirm mother to do anything for herself. She had gotten some mileage out of that—at her own and everyone else's expense. She had become exhausted, bitter, and overwhelmed.

She had always been a big believer in change—and here she was stuck in an insane rut, doing the same thing over and over and expecting a different result. *Thanks, Einstein!* She had known for some time that she was letting herself go because, she told herself, it would be selfish to take care of herself when she couldn't efficiently take care of the others in her life. That was backward: *How can I take care of anyone else unless I first take care of myself?*

"Please, Lord," she prayed, "help me make some changes to restore my relationship with my mom…and with Steve… and with Sally and Tommy…and with my friends at work."

What if tonight, instead of booting up her laptop and plopping down on the couch after dinner, she had stayed and talked with her mom and Steve—not *problem-talk* but just had a normal conversation, played a hand of rummy?

What if she made an effort to find out what it was like for her mother when she had to sell her home, or how it had been for her living in their home? She had never once asked her that since she had moved in. She had never asked her mom how she felt.

Even when her mom was still at Pemberton in rehab, most days Sara would rush in and out as quickly as she could. She would nod as Mom gave her a quick update on her rehab, careful not to ask questions, which would only prolong the misery, and then Sara was out the door. It wasn't that she didn't care. It was that she was overwhelmed (not to mention the fact that she associated Pemberton with the end of her dad's life). Stopping at the facility was just one more thing she had to do and every time she saw her mother she felt like she had more things for Sara to do.

*Of course she did*, Sara thought. *Who wouldn't?* If Sara were in her place, she would have done the same thing. Was it unreasonable that she would request clothes that were more comfortable to wear while undergoing physical therapy? Was it too much to ask for clean clothes to wear each day—especially after being transported by ambulance from your home to the hospital in nothing more than a flimsy nightgown and bedroom slippers?

Sara felt a tidal wave of guilt come over her.

It was strange how she could have gone so long with that anger—that hostility—only to find that once she stopped for a moment, got out of herself, and thought about what her mother was going through, she was simply heartbroken. How cold she had been to her mom. *What could she do now? Apologize?* Mom seemed so angry lately, who knew how she would react.

Maybe she would see if Mom might like to sit out by the flower beds tomorrow evening—just the two of them so they could speak freely. It was a cool in the evenings now, but her mother loved Autumn. She would be game for it...unless she took it as a ploy to get her to exercise, especially after she skipped her therapy today.

It would be good for her to talk to her mother—the way they used to talk. She would tell Mom everything. She would call to chit-chat about the kids and rant and rave about an argument she had with Steve. Of course, Mom always took Steve's side, but in a way that helped Sara realize that maybe she was partly to blame for the argument. Her mom would do basically the same thing her friend Heidy had done; she would say, "Look at it from his perspective.... I'll play Steve. Ready, set...*go!*"

She remembered how, as a child of seven or eight, she had told her mom that she wanted them to come live with her and her own husband and kids after she got married. Her parents would try to stifle their laughter at the naïve comment and say that she would live in her own house and they would live in theirs but that they would always love her and be close enough to come whenever she needed them. They were telling the truth. Her parents had always come when she needed them. They had been there for the triumphs and defeats in life, both big and small—from the second-grade spelling bee in which she received the top honor of a black-and-yellow plastic bumblebee trophy (which to them shined just like an Olympic gold medal) to the night Steve proposed and asked for their blessing. Sara later found out that Steve had not just asked for her father's blessing but for her mother's as well. He had taken them out for lunch without telling Sara and then made them part of the proposal. He asked her at the same spot that her father had asked her mother to marry him—in Hulting Park.

She thought back on that hot summer day. Mom suggested the four of them go for a picnic. Sara wasn't too excited about the idea, but Steve was all for it. So off they went. Her mom had everything they needed: a blanket, fresh strawberries from her garden, and whipped cream, Sara's favorite bologna-and-cheese sandwiches, and a hidden bottle of champagne to pop after the proposal.

Sara had no idea that he was going to propose that day, nor did she know that her folks were in on it, but when Steve got down on one knee she looked over at her parents and they were beaming. When she said, "Yes, of course I will!" her mom slipped the bottle of champagne from the picnic basket along with champagne glasses engraved with their names on them. They were so excited—nearly as excited as the bride-to-be was!

Her mom was in on every detail of the wedding, which was beautiful. Being just out of college and beginning their careers, they couldn't afford a honeymoon, but her parents made it happen for them by presenting them with an all-expenses-paid trip to Hawaii. When Sara said, "You shouldn't have," her mom simply said, "That's what parents do."

That's what *her* parents did, anyway. They were always there with acts of kindness large and small. Sara recalled how her mother, knowing that the two-career family had a busy schedule, would come over a day or two a week and clean their house. Whenever Steve's parents, who lived out of state, would come for a visit, Rose would come over the day before and make up the bed in the guest bedroom with fresh sheets and fluffed pillows. She would dust and vacuum the house and always put a basket in the guest room filled with fresh towels and magazines they might like to read.

Sara remembered telling her mother on one such occasion, "Mom, it's not like our house is a B'n'B!" Her mother just smiled and said there is nothing wrong with making people feel special in your home, especially when they are your parents.

How different things were back then. Mom was so strong, so happy and full of life. Now she was angry and bitter most of the time and never seemed to find much to be happy about.

Sara had tried over the months to help her mother look on the bright side of things—to consider all that she had *not* lost. She was able to go to the same church she had gone to most of her life. Steve had even built a raised garden bed so she could plant flowers and vegetables if she wanted without having to bend over. They had put some of her things from the house that didn't fit into her room in the basement.

But all Mom could do was fix on the negative. She liked to go to the 8:30 a.m. service at church but now had to go to the 11 a.m. service because that was the one that Sara and Steve went to—and that was the one with the praise and worship band that played that "contemporary" music instead of the old standards sung by the choir.

When Steve offered to drop her off at the early service she just made some comment about not wanting to be a burden. And it was a nice gesture bringing those things from the house, but she was in no condition to scale the stairs to the "cellar." And she thanked them for the raised garden, but in the next breath noted that the grass was uneven.

*Have I really tried to understand what she must be feeling? How have I become so cold? It had happened so gradually that she just hadn't noticed.*

She sat up and peered through the opening into the kitchen. Watching her mom and Steve play cards she noticed for the first time how old her mother looked. In her mind's eye she had always seen her mother as the vibrant, smooth-skinned young woman of her childhood.

Yet looking at her now she noticed the lines around her eyes, the paper-thin skin on her hands and the bend of her fingers as she held the playing cards, how her hair had turned from mousy brown to silver without her even noticing.

She looked at her own hands. Even they had lost their youthful luster; she couldn't even remember exactly what her natural hair color was because it was concealed by some concoction the hairdresser mixed together. She stood up and walked over to the entertainment center and picked up the photo of her and Steve's wedding. How young they were—and how young they looked. They were Sally's age! Just out of college. The ceremony was a big affair with all of the traditional wedding customs. Mom made sure she had the something old, something new, something borrowed, and something blue. The something old and borrowed was a cameo pin that had belonged to her mom's great-great-grandmother and which her mom pinned under the bustle of her train. Then there was the beautiful white silk kerchief embroidered with her initials—SAC—embroidered on it in blue. Mom made that wonderful day perfect.

Now almost 25 years and a lifetime later she still felt like she was that girl in the picture. But when she turned and looked at her face in the mirror beside the fireplace it wasn't a girl's face that stared back at her. She noticed the wrinkles around her eyes and how tired she looked. She felt a sudden urgency about time. How quickly the years—25 years—had passed.

Raising the children was just a memory now that they were both young adults away at college. The beginning of her career was a blur. Her father was gone three years already, and in the course of a year her mother had gone from being a strong, independent woman to a frail, elderly lady in need of help for the basic activities of her daily life.

Everyone gets older, of course; that is a part of life. Yet in that moment Sara realized that for each of us there comes a day when we realize that we and those we love will die.

Today was that day for Sara.

# Chapter Fifteen

# 8 p.m.

Rose and Steve were almost finished with their card game, and Rose could still see Sara out in the living room…doing something at the mantelpiece. Looking at pictures? Rose wished Sara would just come in and play one game with them. She remembered their Sunday afternoon tradition when Jack was alive. Sara, Steve, and the kids would meet them at church and then come over to the house after the service for lunch.

The cards would come out around 2:00.

Jack would give his call out "Rummy time!" And do some strange dance and throw down the gauntlet: "Who's ready to lose?"

The grandkids would call back, "You're gonna lose this time, Grandpa!" as they came running in and took their places around the dining room table. They would play until around 6:00 when Rose would fix dinner.

Since moving in with Sara and Steve, she and Steve usually played cards several times a week after dinner. Sara seldom joined in—apparently not interested in reviving the family tradition. She always seemed to have too much work to do or some other commitment.

Steve reminded her so much of Jack. She remembered the day Steve took her and Jack out to lunch to ask for Sara's hand in marriage. It was so wonderful to be included. A groom-to-be usually just met with his beloved's father, but not Steve. He knew how important they both were to Sara. He said, "Since the two of you are as close to what the Bible calls 'one flesh' in marriage as I've ever known, I thought it was only fitting that I ask both of you for your dear daughter's hand in marriage." How could they say anything but yes, yes, yes! She and Jack were overjoyed that their daughter had found such a wonderful man.

Beyond that, Steve even made them part of his proposal. He got all the details of Jack's proposal to Rose so that he could duplicate it with Sara. They were, he said, such wonderful role models for a happy marriage that maybe if he mimicked the important moments in their life he and Sara would enjoy the same kind of marital success. He proposed to Sara on the very spot where Jack proposed to Rose. Rose had been so nervous and excited for Sara that day. Steve had it all planned; he and Sara would stop by to see them. Rose would suggest a picnic at Hulting Park. She would have sandwiches and a basket ready to go with a bottle of champagne stashed away in a secret compartment.

Sara hadn't really seemed too keen on the idea of a picnic, but Rose played her part well and all but forced her daughter into the car. When they got to the park they went to "the spot," and just as she got the blanket spread out, down Steve went on one knee. Rose and Jack had told Sara the story about their engagement so many times when she was a little girl that it didn't take long for her to realize that her future husband was down on one knee in the exact spot where her father had been years before. When Sara looked up at them and realized they were in on it she just started crying.

Rose had found a winery that made special labels for their bottles so she was able to get a bottle of champagne with their names on it. She felt blessed to be able to help out with the wedding planning. She and Sara had so much fun picking out the dress, flowers, and guest gifts.

"Earth to Mom. Mom, do you read me?" Rose looked up to see Steve with his cards in his hand ready to play.

"Loud and clear," she said with a smile. "I guess I was lost in a daydream. You know what they say about us old folks and our reminiscing. I guess it's because there's so much past and so little future." She picked up her cards and fanned them out.

"Well," he said, with a smirk, "if you are rooting around in the past trying to look for a way to beat me, good luck."

"It's not *luck* I need," she told him, "just a little more time." She lowered her voice: "I sure wish Sara would join us."

"You might need luck and time for *that*," he said. "She's working so hard to keep me in the lifestyle to which I've become accustomed. She *is* my Sugar Momma."

They both laughed.

"Well, now, isn't that every mother's dream for her daughter—to be someone's Sugar Momma. Seriously, though, she misses out on so much of life sitting in front of that computer."

"Preaching to the choir there," he said. "I've tried to get her to slow down, but that's just not her. She's a mover and a shaker, Mom. Don't know that we can change it."

"She's going to wear her body and mind out. Just a little fun can go a long way."

"I know, Mom. I have a plan for that."

"Oh?"

He cut his eyes around to make sure Sara was not within earshot of his whisper. "Well, there's a Christian music fest coming to town in a few weeks. It's a huge fall festival, and you know how much Sara loves fall festivals. Used to, anyway. I talked to Tommy and Sally and they're both going to come in so the five of us can go for the day and have some fun. What do you think?"

"I think you are a genius," she said, not bothering to tell him she had the same idea earlier in the day. "In fact," she said, "I'm a big fan of that band Silas Call and their song *Love One Another.*"

"You are?" he said, with one eyebrow raised.

"Mm hmm," she said, just glad she had been able to recall the band and the name of that song. "I'm so glad the children are coming. I miss them, and I know Sara does, too. I don't think I've been such a good stand-in for them showing up just in time to spoil the empty nest."

"Nonsense," he said. "We are glad you are here with us, Mom. You have always been there for *us*. Helping you is the least we can do."

"I never wanted anything in return."

"I know you didn't. Everything you did was out of love for your family."

"All I wanted was just to live my life, preferably in my own home to the very end. The last thing I wanted was to be a burden to my kids."

"You aren't a burden, Rose. I know it's not always easy for you or for us, but we are family and that's what family does."

His kind words brought tears to her eyes and she reached out to touch the back of his hand, but he teased: "Plus, I look like a big stud on the block with two hot chicks living with me! Boy, the gossip mill must be spinning since you moved in."

A few minutes later, she heard the TV shut off and Sara came and stood in the doorway of the kitchen. Rose was hoping she had come to play at least one game with them, but looking up she noticed how tired her daughter looked, the dark circles puffy around her glassy eyes. Sara stood there in the threshold, apparently waiting for them to finish their game.

# Chapter Sixteen

# 10 p.m.

S ara set the wedding picture back on the shelf then walked over to turn off her laptop. She glanced into the kitchen on her way by and saw that Steve and her mother had their end-game faces on. Steve held one card in his hand, and from the expression on his face you might have thought he were about to lay down the winning hand in a million-dollar poker game.

"That's the game, Mom," he said: "RUMMY! Care to be a good sport and congratulate me?"

"Let's not be premature," her mother told him. "We still need to add up the scores, now don't we—to make it *official*?"

Sara put her laptop in the case. She knew that Steve was meticulously adding the points from the round and working his final calculations. She heard him say, "Well, now, I did a count, a recount, and even got out my magnifying glass and figured in the hanging chads…and…*you* won, Mom."

"Now imagine that," her mother said.

"Good game, Mom. Of course, I will want a rematch. Tomorrow night?"

"You're on."

Sara stood in the doorway. "Sounds like you two had a bushel of fun in here, but I'm bushed. I need to be at work by seven. What do you need help with before I head up, Mom?"

"Nothing, honey," she said. "You've been working so hard all evening while we've been in here playing games. Just get some good rest. I'll be okay."

Sara noticed then the pill case on the counter and thought, *Aha, that's one less thing I'll have to worry about when I wake up at 3 a.m.*

But when she moved closer she saw that the pill case was already filled—with two pink pills, one blue pill, and one green pill. It was a little easier for her to say for a fact that she had definitely *not* put the pills in there after coming home from work. "Mother, did you forget to take your pills today?"

"Oh, no, I took them this morning—even before you left for work, and I filled my pill case for tomorrow, too."

*All right, what's going on here?*

"You did?"

"I can still do some things for myself," her mother said, "and the things I *can* do I *should* do."

"You should...." She meant it as a question because she was thinking: *What's come over her?* But it came out sounding more like a statement.

"Yes, I should," her mother agreed.

"Well," Sara said, "at least let me help you get out of those shoes. I know how hard that is for you."

"I'll manage," her mother said.

Her mother gave Steve a hug and they exchanged their nightly farewell:

He said, "Good night, sleep tight, and don't let the bed bugs bite."

Her mother responded, "If they do, I'll send them up to you."

Good grief, Sara thought. She had never understood that bizarre exchange.

"Goodnight, Sara, honey," her mother said. "I love you." Then she turned and walked toward her bedroom.

Sara followed her mother into her room, just off the kitchen, but it took her a good long time to make it in to her bedroom. Her step was light but anything but sure, and she was really favoring her right leg so her limp was as bad as Sara had ever seen it.

When she noticed that Sara had followed her in, she said, "Honey, I can get my own shoes off tonight. You look tired. Why don't you go up and get some sleep. I'll be fine."

"It's okay, Mom," she said, trying to soften her tone. She felt tense—very aware of how strongly she reacted to her mother—even though her mother was not asking for anything. *Why am I responding to her as though I am being inconvenienced? Mom had actually been very sweet and considerate all evening….*

Her mother just looked at her and said, "You've done so much for me, Sara."

"Then taking your shoes off won't add anything to your tab," she said.

Her mother looked at her again as if she were weighing whether to fight or surrender and let Sara help her get her shoes off. In the end, she chose to flee. She said, "I have to run to the powder room, if you don't mind waiting a minute?"

"Fine, Mother."

Alone in the room, Sara recognized the song playing on her mother's radio—*There is a Reason* by Caedmon's Call. It was disarming to hear "contemporary" music coming from her mother's radio. *How Great Thou Art* was more her mother's speed—that and radio preachers of the red-faced hellfire-and-brimstone sort who were constantly having to mop the sweat off their necks with monogrammed handkerchiefs.

175

The song faded and the smooth rich voice of the KLOVE evening disc jockey came on: "That song goes to Jennie Benter, co-host of our morning show, whose mother passed away suddenly this morning. Our thoughts and prayers are with Jen and her family during this time."

Just then Sara's own mother emerged from the bathroom.

"Oh, Sara honey," she said, "I'm so sorry you had to wait. I'm just not as spry as I used to be."

"That's okay, Mom. Let me help you get your shoes off."

"I bet you never thought when you were a little girl that one day your mother would be such an old woman who couldn't get her own shoes on and off."

Sara worked the orthopedic shoes they had fitted Rose with off of her feet and pulled the footies on. She recalled her conversation with Heidy, who had said: *"Imagine what it's like to walk in her shoes—having to have somebody do things that you have done for yourself your whole life...."*

*What if I walked in these shoes? How will it be when I do walk in these shoes?*

"I know it hasn't been easy on you, Mom."

"Well, nobody ever said it was going to be easy—especially when you get well past your three score and 10."

"What nightgown do you want to wear?"

"The one I'll find as soon as you get on to bed," her mother said. "It's way past your bedtime."

Now it was Sara's turn to decide whether to fight or flee or surrender. *Have I been so impatient with her that she no longer wants my help with anything?* It felt so strange to be told that she wasn't needed. It had seemed for the past year that her mother had needed so much of her help and now.... *What's come over her?*

"I insist," her mother said. "I think all that blood, sweat, toil, and tears I've put in at that physical therapy might be paying off. I'm feeling stronger." She made a gesture as if she were flexing her biceps.

The nightly "tuck-in" ritual (as Steve called it) had consumed 20–30 minutes a night for the past six months. It was a slow process that involved taking off her mother's shoes then helping her into her nightgown. Sara had become very adept at helping her mother change without having her dignity compromised. *I don't want to flash you,* her mother always said. For a while it had been funny and helped to alleviate some of the awkwardness she felt having to help her mother dress—*before* Sara's exhaustion and anger and bitterness and whatever else had gotten the best of her.

The process went something like this: Her mother would sit on the edge of the bed and Sara would remove her shoes and place the gown over her head. Her mother would then slip her arms out of her shirt and bra and Sara would remove the clothing through the top of the gown, then her mother would button the top button. Then Sara would turn off the lights as she left the room.

Sara thought back. This must be the first night in six months that they had not done the ritual. "Are you sure, Mom?"

"Yes, honey, I am."

"Goodnight, Mom," Sara whispered as she turned and walked out of the room, pulling the door to, but not shut, behind her.

Upstairs Steve was already in bed reading. "Did you get Mom all snuggled in for the night?"

"Well, she kind of wanted to tuck herself in tonight."

"Really?" he asked, looking up from the hardback thriller he was reading.

"That's what I said. She said it was time for her to do what she could for herself."

"That's music to your ears, isn't it?"

"What's that supposed to mean, Steve?"

His smiled faded. "Why so touchy, honey? You know you don't have to be so serious all the time."

"Oh, don't I?" she asked.

"No, you don't. Your mom can do a lot of things for herself. There are some people whose parents can't do *anything* for themselves."

"Is that supposed to make me feel better?"

"I guess it didn't work," he said, smiling again. Trying to bring her back down from what he called her *high horse of seriosity.*

"That's easy for you to say, Steve," she snapped. She tried to calm the sick feeling in her stomach. "You're not the one who has to take care of everything for her. *I am.* I'm the one who has to organize her pills, take her to the doctor, coordinate Lily's schedule, help her get undressed at night."

"Sweetie, listen, I know you do a lot for your mom. But sometimes, well, maybe you do *too much.* Remember what they told us at when she was at Pemberton. Dr. Peterson, I think it was, said, 'Encourage Mrs. Barnes to be as self-sufficient as she can possibly be. Do *not* do for her things that she can do for herself.' Remember?"

"Vaguely," she said, remembering it as though it were yesterday.

"Having Mom here with us is really a blessing...."

Sara lowered her eyebrows, and he said, "Every blessing in this life is mixed, Sara. But, I mean, look at my parents. They're 800 miles away. Sometimes it doesn't even feel like I know them anymore. Your mom is right here. You get to see her whenever you want. I wish I had that with my folks. I'm closer to your mom than I am to my own."

"You and Mom are pretty chummy, all right."

"She's a lot of fun, just like you are, though not so much lately. You've become so serious, Sara," he told her. "Well, I'll say this and then I'll shut up. I just think that sometimes you miss out on opportunities to really enjoy time with your mom because you are so busy with the list of tasks you have to get done."

Sara rolled her eyes. "Oh brother. I spend time with her every day. What are you trying to say?"

"I'm just saying that tonight I had a great time playing cards with Mom while you sat on the couch and worked. I know you have a lot going on at work, but every once in a while you could shut off the computer and spend a little *quality* time with your mom. None of us knows what tomorrow brings, Sara. We're not going to have Mom around forever, which is why I try to make the most of the time I have with her."

His words trailed off.

"I know," she said. She went into the bathroom and brushed her teeth, trying to let the conversation end. A few minutes later she was in bed with her back turned to Steve.

"Goodnight, honey," he said as he turned out the light.

"Goodnight." Sara stared at the ceiling, tears flowing down her cheeks.

## Chapter Seventeen

# 10 p.m.

R ose could tell by the smirk on Steve's face that he was about to lay down the final card that would win him the game. His demeanor reminded her of Jack. He used to be so intense when he played cards. He always played to win, sure, but he never hurt anyone's feelings while he squashed their hopes of ever being the champ.

"That's the game, Mom," he said: "RUMMY! Care to be a good sport and congratulate me?"

"Let's not be premature," Rose told him with a smile. They both knew that laying down your cards is only part of the game. They still had to count the suits she had in her hand and then add up the total points. Looking at her cards, she knew she was almost certainly the winner. With a clever smile she said, "We still need to add up the scores, now don't we—to make it *official*."

Steve was meticulous, and it took him a full five minutes to work his calculations. He looked up at her and shook his head. "Well, now, I did a count, a recount, and even got out my magnifying glass and figured in the hanging chads... and...*you* won, Mom."

"Now imagine that," she told him.

"Good game, Mom. Of course, I will want a rematch. Tomorrow night?"

"You're on," she told him.

She hoped now that he had gotten the big contract he would still have a little time for an occasional card game in the evening after dinner. It was something she looked forward to—that, and chatting over coffee in the morning. For all she knew he would end up sitting in front of the TV with his own computer for hours on end each night.

Sara was standing in the doorway still, leaning against the doorjamb as though on the verge of collapse. The bags under her eyes worried Rose.

Sara said, "Sounds like you two had a bushel of fun in here, but I'm bushed. I need to be at work by seven. What do you need help with before I head up, Mom?"

"Nothing, honey," Rose told her, trying to sound confident. "You've been working so hard all evening while we've been in here playing games. Just get some good rest. I'll be okay."

Then Sara took a step toward the pill case on the counter. "Mother, did you forget to take your pills today?"

"Oh, no, I took them this morning—even before you left for work, and I filled my pill case for tomorrow, too." Rose amazed herself with how proud she felt for accomplishing such a minor task.

"You did?"

"I can still do some things for myself," Rose told her daughter, "and the things I *can* do I *should* do."

"You should," Sara said, with a puzzled expression on her face.

"Yes, I should," Rose agreed.

"Well," Sara said, "at least let me help you get out of those shoes. I know how hard that is for you."

"I'll manage," she said, again trying to sound convincing but feeling some apprehension of her abilities.

Rose gave Steve a hug and they exchanged their nightly farewell:

He said, "Good night, sleep tight, and don't let the bed bugs bite."

Rose responded, "If they do, I'll send them up to you."

Sara rolled her eyes. That weird exchange was something of an inside joke between Rose and Steve that began one night shortly after she moved in. She and Steve were sitting at the table sharing favorite memories from childhood. Rose had mentioned that this had been a nightly exchange between her and her mother each evening when she was a little girl. That same night right before she went into her room Steve said his normal goodnight and then added the rest of the phrase. She answered him back with the "If they do…" part and they had been saying it ever since.

Rose noticed how haggard her daughter looked. *Living here, I've put 10 years on her*, Rose thought. Her eyes were bloodshot and her coloring was off.

"Goodnight, Sara, honey," she told her. "I love you." Then she turned and walked toward her bedroom, not waiting for a reply. So many times lately when she told Sara she loved her all she got in reply was silence or a shrug.

Her hip was burning, so she took her time, and it wasn't until she was in her room that she noticed that Sara had followed her in. "Honey," she told her, "I can get my own shoes off. You look tired. Why don't you go up and get some sleep. I'll be fine."

"It's *okay,* Mom," Sara said. She seemed perturbed.

Rose thought, *I can manage, I hope.* She had a troublesome feeling, as if her growing needs had put an undue amount of pressure on Sara, so who could blame the girl for being a little perturbed, not to mention worn to a frazzle! When she first moved in with them, Rose just needed help with her shoes. She could take care of the rest of her clothes; however, in the past few months she had gotten used to accepting more help with her clothes. Most days she needed a lot of help with dressing especially on those days when her pain and the arthritis in her hands impaired her mobility. She wondered how much more Sara could take.... Rose was keenly aware that her needs were becoming more and more pressing as the months passed.

She wished she could move like she did when she was younger. She had always been a fast-walker. She was busy and couldn't burn daylight dawdling around. At work when she whizzed by on her way to make copies or a fresh pot of coffee her boss would call out from his office, "Hey, slow down, Rose; all that racing around is making *me* tired." She would remind him that if she slowed down not only her own work but half of *his* wouldn't get done.

The older women in the office always reminisced about how they had once been fleet-footed girls, too, and admonished Rose to enjoy her speedy legs while she was young. She remembered thinking to herself how silly those women were, thinking that even 25 years before they had probably never moved fast.

Rose looked at Sara and said, "You've done so much for me, Sara." It was almost embarrassing to have to admit that out loud.

"Then taking off your shoes won't add anything to your tab," Sara said.

Rose really wanted to insist that Sara go to bed, but her daughter was stubborn—a trait she had come by honestly enough—and would take that as a challenge. Rose excused herself and went into the bathroom. She was half thinking that Sara might just go up to bed. She was practically dead on her feet.

A few minutes later, she was back in her bedroom and Sara was leaning against the footboard of her bed with a very sad expression on her face. Maybe it was just fatigue. There was a fine line between the two sometimes.

"Oh, Sara honey," she said, "I'm so sorry you had to wait. I'm just not as spry as I used to be."

"That's okay, Mom. Let me help you get your shoes off."

"I bet you never thought when you were a little girl that one day your mother would be such an old woman who couldn't get her own shoes on and off." Rose said trying to make light of the situation.

Sara took off her shoes, very gently, and Rose was thankful that she had a daughter who cared for her so much.

"I know it hasn't been easy on you, Mom."

"Well, nobody ever said it was going to be easy—especially when you get well past your three score and 10."

"What nightgown do you want to wear?"

"The one I'll find as soon as you get on to bed," Rose told her. "It's way past your bedtime." Sara just looked at her and then she let out a big breath, and Rose said, "I insist. I think all that blood, sweat, toil, and tears I've put in at that physical therapy might be paying off. I'm feeling stronger." She amused herself by making a gesture as if she were flexing her biceps.

"Are you sure, Mom?" Rose noted that Sara was not all that amused. Bad subject since she skipped out on therapy today.

"Yes, honey, I am."

Rose got herself undressed and into her nightgown. It was none too easy, but she was able to do it, and she felt a little better, if a little more exhausted, for the effort. *The things I can do for myself, I should do for myself. And I will,* she told herself. *And the things I can do for Sara, I should do for Sara. There will come a day, if the Lord should tarry, when I won't be able to do anything for myself. Until then, I shall.*

She lay in the darkness staring up waiting for the pain medication she had taken while in the bathroom to kick in.

She thought about her day. *Another long one.* It seemed most days she was alone in the company of her memories. But today she had gotten a double dose of Steve and a single shot of Lily, but not all that much of Sara.

So many memories. So many years distilled into a few hours of cherished moments. How quickly her life had passed. How can a moment of time seem so long and a lifetime so brief? All those years had led up to this moment in time when she, an old woman, Jack Barnes's widow, needed to be cared for by her children.

*How did I get to this point—and so quickly?*

Her time with Jack.

Caring for the girls.

Helping them as young wives and mothers with their own families.

Jack's illness.

Her slip and fall.

Selling the house.

Moving in with Sara and Steve.

As her grandfather use to say, "Life happens in the blink of an eye." Her thoughts trailed off.

She thought about how strained her relationship with Sara had become. And she saw behind it a lot of anger she was taking out on Sara...when in fact it wasn't Sara she was angry at, but Jack Barnes. No, it certainly wasn't his fault that he was stricken with Alzheimer's, but he had left her...left her alone to handle the decisions about his care during his illness...left her alone to figure out what to do once he died...left her alone to mourn the loss of their home and memories.

They had always been a team, making decisions together, overcoming challenges together. And alas she was left to face the biggest challenges of her life all alone.

And, well, truth to tell, she was angry at Carol, too. Carol was a little too content to let Sara shoulder all the burdens alone. And, since she was being honest with herself, she had to admit that she was a little angry with herself, too—for not doing all she could for herself and for taking out all of her frustration on Sara.

*How much time do we waste every day being angry and upset with those we love over petty issues? Doesn't love transcend all the little things that get us so worked up?*

In the blink of an eye her life had changed. In the blink of an eye the girls were grown with their own families. In the blink of an eye Jack was diagnosed with Alzheimer's and in another blink, he was gone. In the blink of an eye three years had passed since his death. In the blink of an eye her home was gone and she was dependent on her daughter.

With tears spilling from her eyes she began to pray silently: "Heavenly Father, I pray you give me a peace in my soul. Help me to grieve my losses and not take out my frustrations on my daughter. Give me healing for my pain and relief from my ailments. Give me the patience to take my time and understand my limitations. Dear Lord, comfort me in my losses and give me the strength to do more, and let your grace be made perfect in my weakness. Help me to show more grace and mercy to those around me and to enjoy the time I have with them. Help me not drive a wedge between my daughters, Sara and Carol. Lord, I know that you are merciful and your grace is enough for me, but I ask, please Lord, give me a sign so that I'm not such a burden. Thank you for loving me in spite of myself. Amen."

Moved by her thoughts she rolled over and turned the light on and pulled a piece of paper out of the drawer next to her bed and wrote down three words.

REMEMBER TO LOVE.

This was not a reminder of inward love; she always loved her family. It was rather to remind her every day to be more loving outwardly to those around her.

# Chapter Eighteen

# 10:45 p.m.

S ara lay there thinking about Jen from KLOVE. Last night that woman had no idea that it would be the last night of her life that she would go to bed with her mother alive on earth.

She wondered when was the last time Jen had seen her mother or spoken to her on the phone. And on that occasion had she told her mother how she felt about her? Or had she meant to call her mother but gotten busy and decided to call her today—only to find out that there was no today for her mother and that there never would be again?

In that moment Sara was overcome by an overwhelming flood of emotion. *How much time do we waste every day being angry and upset with those we love over petty issues? Doesn't love transcend all the little things that get us so worked up?*

Sara reflected on the picture from her parents' 50th anniversary. How long Dad had suffered but how quickly he was gone. In the blink of an eye he was gone. In the blink of an eye five years had passed. In the blink of an eye Mom would be gone as well.

With tears spilling from her eyes she began to pray silently: "Heavenly Father, help me to appreciate Mom. Give her healing for her ailments and give me the patience to care for her. Dear Lord, comfort her in her losses and assist me in the things I need to do to care for her. Help me to show her more grace and mercy. And, Lord, please help heal my relationship with Carol. Thank you for loving me. Amen."

She got out of bed and headed for the door.

"Is everything okay?" Steve asked as she reached the door.

She cleared her throat, said, "Sure. I just forgot to do something. I'll be right back up. Just go to sleep." She closed the door behind her and went back downstairs, the sound of her footsteps echoing through the dark house. She made her way through the kitchen wiping the tears from her eyes. She took a deep breath as she slowly opened the door to her mom's room.

"Is that you, Sara? Is everything okay?"

"Yes, Mom, everything's fine." Sara's voice softened as she continued. "I forgot to tell you that I love you." She paused. "I do love you, Mom."

"I know you do, honey. I love you, too."

# Chapter Nineteen

# 10:45 p.m.

Rose turned off the light and lay back down and listened to the sound of footsteps coming down the stairs. Sara and Steve had gone up to bed a while ago. She hoped everything was all right. She heard the footsteps come through the living room and kitchen and stop at her door. She took a deep breath as her door slowly opened and Sara entered the room.

"Is that you, Sara? Is everything okay?"

"Yes, Mom, everything's fine." Sara's voice softened as she continued. "I forgot to tell you that I love you." She paused. "I do love you, Mom."

"I know you do, honey. I love you, too."

Rose could feel the lump in her throat as the tears began to flow down her cheeks. She said a silent prayer of thanks to God for listening to her and for loving her in spite of herself.

# Epilogue

"I love you."
"I love you, too."

This is a very common exchange between two people that can be used to express a feeling of affection, adoration, romance, intimacy, and care. It is an expression of intimacy in a relationship, an illustration of our connectedness to others. It is a customary phrase we utter daily to our spouse, children, parents, and close friends.

*But what does it really mean to love and be loved?*

In this story you have been able to walk in the shoes of both mother and daughter as they navigate through a day of routines, responsibilities, and relationships.

In Sara we find the dutiful daughter, devoted mother and wife, the faithful sister, friend, and co-worker. She passes most days so engrossed in her roles and responsibilities that she doesn't have a moment to spare thinking about herself and her own needs. It is ironic that despite all she gives to those around her the only view she has is the one of herself reflected back at her.

We can relate to Sara because most of us either *know* a Sara or *are* a Sara.

In spending a day with Rose, on the other hand, we are transported to the other side of caregiving, the side that caregivers, caught up in the whirlwind of expectations and responsibilities, rarely consider or understand, the side where there is a different expression of the human condition.

It is on Rose's side of caregiving where we come to see the profound experience of loss—loss of independence, of abilities, of dignity, and of loved ones who can be encountered only through faded memories.

In a world full of to-do lists and seemingly never-ending responsibilities, it is difficult to appreciate what it is like to walk in the shoes of the person on the other side of the caregiving interchange. Most days we look at our life in a mirror that reflects only our stress and frustration.

Just think…

- What our life would be like if we made the choice to evaluate our daily life from both sides of the mirror?
- What would happen if at various points during our day we made an effort to consider our reactions and interactions with our children, spouse, friends, co-workers, and aging parents not from our own perspective but from *theirs*?
- How many misunderstandings and hurt feelings could be avoided if we stopped for just a moment to think about the other person?

It can be difficult for us even to imagine these things, especially when we are caring for an aging loved one who requires attention physically, mentally, and psycho-socially. Taking the other person's perspective is not easy but it can be very rewarding.

Caring for a loved one is a choice that some of us make and some of us don't. There is a great deal of joy and blessing when we care for our aging loved ones. If as care-givers, however, we do not access the resources we need or ask for help the pressure can become unbearable. Soon the internal pressure—the anger, frustration, bitterness, resent-ment, and sheer exhaustion—release externally on those we love. Caregivers and those they care for can feel isolated by their circumstances, as if they are the only one who has ever experienced their situation.

So, then, what does "I love you" mean when spoken at the end of the day between a caregiver and the one being cared for?

Perhaps it means a gesture of reconciliation and a reminder that at the end of the day there is a bond between people who love each other that cannot be broken by circumstances.

Caring for an aging parent can be a very rewarding gift that we not only give to someone we love, but to ourselves. This is not to suggest that there will not be difficult times or challenging situations. There will be. Nor is it to say that we are perfect and that there will never be any misunderstand-ings or hurt feelings. There will be.

Because inevitably the day will come when we will look into our own mirror and the reflection looking back at us will be that of Rose....

# Acknowledgments

This book took me on a heartfelt journey of amazing introspection. It is the product of years of both professional and personal experience and character compilations of many family caregivers and the family members they have cared for rolled into a day in the life of a mother and daughter. I could not have done any of it without the love and encouragement of so many people; I would like to acknowledge some of the persons specifically.

My incredible husband and best friend, Paul Cutler, who gave support, love and much needed hugs while I experienced an overabundance of emotional highs and lows during the creation of these characters and their stories; or as he sometimes referred to them – the little people in my head. I am grateful for the prayers, unconditional love and creative contribution to the process.

My Mom, Geri Salach, who has always believed in me no matter what. The caring, gentle parts of Rose are written from experiencing my mothers' remarkable character and role model in my life.

The amazingly talented Michele Moroney for another creative cover design. Her willingness to share her creative gift for my books is such a blessing.

Scott Philip Stewart, Ph.D., from Christian Author Services, who provided key editorial assistance and valuable insight and perspective to my materials.

Special thanks to Heidy Montgomery, Jan Hutchinson, Molly Martinez and Caryn Amster and Aunt Josie Supela, for always being there to lend an ear when I needed to be heard and a gentle voice to give me honest and loving feedback.

Thanks to the many family, friends and professionals who supported, prayed and listened to my stories over and over again with patience, encouragement and love. I am truly blessed to have so many wonderful and supportive people in my life.

Most importantly I want to thank my savior, Jesus Christ, through whom I can do all things! I am grateful for being led by the Spirit to write this book and for the many people He put in my path to help me along the way.

# Finding Resources for Caregivers

If you or someone you know is caring for an aging loved one, you can access resources online at the following sites:

www.ifiwalkedinhershoes.com
www.alongcomesgrandpa.com
www.aginginfousa.org
www.caregiverlife.com

Caregiver support or small group leaders and facilitators can find resources to promote in group discussion on this and related topics at:

www.caregivingonline.com

For information on upcoming workshops and programs presented by author Sue Salach or to contact the author to coordinate a program for your organization or group visit:

www.caregiverseminars.com

Printed in the United States
205045BV00001B/151-600/P

9 781606 476130